D1507212

KEYS TO THE KINGDOM
KINGDOM

Lady Friday

GARTH NIX

KEYS TO THE KINGDOM

BOOK FIVE
Lady Friday

SCHOLASTIC INC.

New York Toronto London Auckland Sydney
Mexico City New Delhi Hong Kong Buenos Aires

No part of this publication may be reproduced, stored in a retrieval system, or transmitted in any form or by any means, electronic, mechanical, photocopying, recording, or otherwise, without written permission of the publisher. For information regarding permission, write to Scholastic Inc., Attention: Permissions Department, 557 Broadway, New York, NY 10012.

This book was originally published in hardcover by Scholastic Press in 2007.

ISBN-13: 978-0-439-43658-8
ISBN-10: 0-439-43658-3

12 11 10 9 8 7 6 5 4 3   9 10 11 12 13/0

Printed in the U.S.A.   40

First Scholastic paperback printing, February 2008

The display type was set in Dalliance and Albertus.
The text type was set in Sabon.
Book design by Steve Scott

To Anna, Thomas, Edward, and
all my family and friends;
and with particular thanks to all
the staff at Scholastic in the USA,
Allen & Unwin in Australia,
and HarperCollins UK

KEYS TO THE KINGDOM

Lady Friday

Prologue

Leaf woke with a start and sat up in bed. For a moment she was disoriented, because she wasn't in her own bed. No band poster stared back at her from the wall at the foot of the bed, because there was no wall. The bedside table was missing too, and on the other side there were no winking red eyes from her four-foot-high troll clock, the one she'd made with her brother, Ed, several years before for a school science project.

She wasn't in her normal sleeping clothes either: a band T-shirt and tracksuit pants. Instead she was wearing an ankle-length pale blue nightshirt of soft flannel, something she would never have chosen to put on herself.

The room she was in was much bigger than her bedroom, and there were eight other beds. The closer ones definitely had people asleep in them, because Leaf could see bodies under the covers and the tops of their heads. The other beds were probably occupied as well.

It looked like a hospital. . . .

Leaf suddenly became a lot more awake. She tried to

jump out of the bed, but her legs wouldn't hold her up, and it turned into more of a slither onto the floor. Clawing at the bedclothes, she got herself upright and leaned against the mattress while she tried to work out what was going on.

Slowly it all started to come back. Very slowly, as if her recent memory was broken and her brain was having trouble putting all the pieces back together.

Leaf remembered visiting her friend Arthur in the East Area Hospital. He'd told her about the House that was the epicenter of the Universe, and how he had been chosen to become the Rightful Heir to the Architect — not because he was born to be or anything like that, but because he'd been the right person at the right time. (Or the wrong person at the wrong time, depending on how you looked at it.) The Architect was apparently the creator of everything. She'd made not only the House but also the whole Universe beyond it, including the Earth.

Arthur had told Leaf about all this, and about Mister Monday and Grim Tuesday, two of the Trustees who had betrayed the missing Architect and refused to execute her Will. But before he'd finished, a huge wave had come from nowhere, washing them both into an ocean that wasn't even on Earth. Arthur had been carried away even farther out on the strange sea, but Leaf had been picked up by a ship, the *Flying Mantis*. . . .

"The *Mantis*," whispered Leaf. Even a whisper sounded loud in the quiet room. There was no noise at all from the sleeping people in the other beds. Not even a snore. Suddenly Leaf wondered if they were actually dead rather than sleeping, and she stared at the closest bed to check. She could only see the top of the person's head, just a tuft of hair — not enough to figure out whether it was a man or a woman. But after a few seconds Leaf was relieved to see the blanket rise and fall slightly. Man or woman, the person was breathing very slowly.

"I sailed on the *Mantis*," Leaf whispered to herself. It was all coming back. She had sailed the Border Sea in the House for six weeks. She'd become one of the crew . . . then the pirates had attacked. Her friend Albert had been killed. . . .

Leaf shut her eyes. She didn't want to have that memory come into her head. But at least she had helped Arthur defeat the pirates, and had kicked their leader Feverfew's head into a pool of Nothing-infused mud. Then they'd gone back to Port Wednesday and caught an elevator to . . .

"The Front Door," said Leaf. "Doorstop Hill. The Lieutenant Keeper . . ."

She and Arthur had tried to get back home through the Front Door in the Lower House, but there'd been a problem.

The Lieutenant Keeper wouldn't let Arthur through the Door . . . and then . . . there was the meeting with Dame Primus where they'd found out that the Skinless Boy had taken over Arthur's identity back on Earth, preventing him from going home. But there hadn't been anything to stop Leaf from going home. She'd *wanted* to go home, after what had happened, but it wasn't as easy as that.

"I volunteered to banish the Skinless Boy," Leaf muttered, in amazement at herself. "I must have been crazy."

But she *had* succeeded in finding the source of the Skinless Boy's power, and she *had* managed to deliver it to Suzy Turquoise Blue, against all odds. But along the way she had been infected with the mind-control mold that would let the Skinless Boy control her every thought and action. . . .

Memories joined up and stitched themselves together. Leaf frowned in concentration as she tried to work out what must have happened. Suzy had obviously delivered the sorcerous pocket the Skinless Boy had been made with to Arthur, and he must have used the pocket to destroy the dangerous Nithling. If either one had failed, Leaf wouldn't be conscious now. She'd be a brain-dead slave of the Skinless Boy.

But Leaf didn't feel particularly victorious, because she'd finally remembered that this wasn't the first time she'd regained consciousness after being affected by the mind-control fungus.

"There was a tent hospital . . . a temporary one," Leaf said. Talking to herself helped bring back the details. "I was vomiting up the sludge left from the mold. . . ."

Leaf groaned and pushed her knuckles into her temples as she remembered something else. The nurse had told her she'd been in a coma for a week. From Thursday afternoon to Friday morning.

But how long ago was that? she wondered. *I must have gone back into a coma, or . . .*

Leaf stopped knuckling her temples and let her forehead smack into the mattress. She leaned back and did it again. It was a bad habit, but she couldn't help herself. She always beat her head — with something soft — when things went wrong.

The last thing she remembered was the nurse pointing out an approaching female doctor. And then she'd said the terrible words:

"Doctor Friday, imagine that! We call her Lady Friday on the wards. . . ."

Leaf vaguely recalled feeling an awful sensation of fear swarm up inside her as an incredibly beautiful woman had approached with a whole host of people behind her . . . but everything after that was blank.

Doctor Friday — who clearly had come from the House and really was the Trustee called Lady Friday — must have done something to her.

Maybe I've lost even more time, Leaf thought. *Anything could have happened. To Arthur. To my parents. To Ed. Anything.*

A noise from the end of the room startled Leaf. She froze for a moment, dropped down behind the bed, then crawled to the end to take a proper look around. Someone was pushing open the double-swing doors at one end of the room. First something slid through the gap. It took Leaf a moment to recognize it as a bucket being pushed along with a mop. The person who was doing the pushing eased through the doors and kicked them shut behind her with a practiced heel.

She looked very normal and human: a middle-aged woman with downcast eyes and sensibly tied-back hair, wearing a green smock, green overalls, and white rubber boots. Leaf was relieved by that. If the woman were six foot four and strikingly good-looking, then she would probably be a Denizen and that would mean Leaf was back in the House.

After coming through the door, the cleaner stopped for a moment to dip the mop in the bucket and then started mopping a path about six feet wide down the middle of the room. She didn't look particularly observant, but there was no way she could avoid seeing the empty bed.

Leaf looked around for something she might be able to use as a weapon, and tried to gauge whether her legs would support her if she attempted to stand up again. She felt incredibly weak, a result of being in bed for so long, but fear lent her strength. There was something about all the sleeping bodies in the beds in the rest of the ward that really freaked her out. The room just didn't feel like a normal hospital, and Leaf knew it had something to do with Lady Friday.

Her quick scan confirmed that it wasn't a normal hospital. There was none of the usual equipment on the walls or near the beds — the oxygen outlets, the call buttons, and all that kind of stuff. In fact, all there was in the whole room were the simple beds and the people sleeping their strange sleep.

She looked back at the cleaner, who unfortunately chose that exact moment to look up. They both stared for a moment, gazes locked, then the cleaner gave a suppressed shriek and dropped her mop.

Leaf staggered upright and tried to make a dash to grab the mop. Even though she could barely stay upright and didn't feel like much of a threat, the cleaner shrieked again and backed away. Leaf almost fell over the bucket but did manage to get the mop, stand up, and brandish it like a staff.

"Don't . . . don't do anything!" said the woman in a forced whisper. She was clearly afraid — but not of Leaf. She was looking back at the door. "You have to get back into bed. She's on her way!"

Leaf lowered the mop. "Who's on her way? What is this place?"

"Her!" said the cleaner. "Quick! Get back in bed. You have to pretend to be like the others. Just copy what they do."

"Why?"

The cleaner shuddered.

"You have to. If you don't . . . she'll do something to your head. I only saw it once. Someone like you, awake when he shouldn't have been! She used that mirror of hers, and I saw . . . I saw . . ."

"What!?"

"I saw the life drained out of him," whispered the woman. She was pale as cotton wool now, and shaking. "She shone that little mirror, and I saw . . . something . . . come out of his head. Then she tilted the mirror to her mouth and she —"

The woman stopped talking and swallowed convulsively, unable to continue.

"There must be a way out," said Leaf fiercely. She pointed at the other door, the one opposite where the cleaner had come in. "Where does that go?"

"To the pool," whispered the woman. "Her pool. You have to get back into bed. Please, please, I don't want to see it happen again!"

Leaf hesitated, then thrust the mop back at the cleaner, who gripped it like she might grab a lifeline. Then Leaf started to walk down toward the far door.

"No!" shrieked the cleaner. "She'll see the empty bed! It's Friday, nothing is the same here on Friday!"

Leaf tried to keep walking, but her legs gave way. She fell down on her hands and knees. Before she could get back up, the cleaner was lifting her up under the armpits and carrying her back to bed. Leaf struggled, but she was just too weak.

"Copy the sleepers," gasped the cleaner. "It's your only chance. Follow them."

"Where?" snapped Leaf. She was furious that her body wouldn't obey her properly.

"They go into the pool," said the cleaner. "Only it's not the pool. . . . I'm not supposed to have seen. I'm only supposed to clean the floor ahead of her. But I watched once, through the louvers in the change room. . . ."

"Do they come back?"

"I don't know," whispered the woman. "Not here. It was only twenty a month, that's all, from when I first started here. That was thirty years ago. But the whole place was filled up this week. She must be taking thousands of people this time."

"What people? Who? From the hospitals?"

"Hush!" exclaimed the woman. She dragged the covers up over Leaf and rushed back to her mop, pushing the bucket almost to the next door. As she frantically dabbed at the floor, the cleaner called back over her shoulder, "She's coming!"

Leaf reluctantly lay flat but she turned her head so she could see the door through her half-closed eyes. After a minute, she heard heavy footsteps, and the door was flung open. Two very tall, very handsome men in charcoal-gray business suits and trench coats stormed through. Leaf recognized their type immediately. Superior Denizens, their coats humped at the shoulders, evidence of the wings beneath.

Behind the two Denizens came the beautiful woman Leaf had seen in the tent hospital. Lady Friday was very tall, made taller by her stiletto-heeled boots that were set with rubies. She wore a gold robe that shimmered as she walked, sending bright reflections dancing everywhere, and a hat studded with small pieces of colored glass, or maybe even small diamonds, which caught the golden light and intensified it, so brightly that it was very difficult to look too long upon Friday's face.

The Trustee held something small in her right hand that was brighter still, so bright it was impossible to look at. Leaf had to completely shut her eyes, but even so, the light burst through her lids and sent a stab of pain across the bridge of her nose.

With her eyes screwed shut, Leaf couldn't see what happened next. But she heard it. The soft footfall of many bare feet, strange after the *click-clack* of the Denizen's shoes and Friday's boot heels, but just as loud.

Leaf waited till she was sure Friday had passed, then she looked again.

The whole room was full of sleepwalkers following Friday. A great line of people in blue nightgowns shambled along with their eyes shut, many in the classic pose with their arms outstretched ahead, others looking so relaxed they could barely stay upright and keep moving.

They were all fairly old. Most of the men were bald or had silver or gray hair, and looked to Leaf like they must be on the wrong side of seventy. It was harder to tell with the women, but they were probably on the far side of that age as well. None of them were exactly ancient, and they were all walking, but none of them could be described as even middle-aged.

Leaf watched them pass while she tried to work out what to do. Hundreds of people went by and Leaf started to think she could just let them all go, hide under the bed, and then sneak out. But then she saw two more Denizens, chivying the sleepers like sheepdogs. Several minutes and a few hundred people later, another two Denizens came by. Given that, there were bound to be even more Denizens guarding the end of the line.

Then Leaf saw something that made up her mind in an instant.

Her aunt Mango was in the line. Sound asleep and walking with a slight, sleepy smile.

Leaf jerked up, then caught herself doing it and somehow managed to lie back down just before the next two Denizens came into the room.

Aunt Mango was almost like a second mother to her and Ed. She'd lived with Leaf's family for years, as long as Leaf could remember. She was Leaf's mother's older sister, but acted more like her younger, somewhat helpless sibling. Leaf wasn't sure about her history, but Aunt Mango had either been born with a slight intellectual disability or something had happened to her. She was kind and loving, but completely hopeless with the everyday chores of life, and her enthusiastic incompetence needed constant supervision. Sometimes she really irritated Leaf, but Aunt Mango had always been there for her, to tell her stories, to listen to her troubles, to comfort her.

Leaf watched her aunt till she went through the far door.

I have to go with them now, she thought. *Aunt Mango isn't any good with big stuff; she wouldn't have a hope alone. But I've got nothing. No weapon. No way of getting in touch with anyone useful. No House sorcery. . . .*

Her hand twitched. She stopped the movement, then stealthily slid her fingers up to her neck, feeling for something that she really, really hoped was still there, because if it was, then she actually *did* have something sorcerous and potentially useful.

Leaf's fingers found the braided dental floss necklace and followed it, finally closing on the tiny carved whalebone disc that Arthur had given her. The Mariner's medallion.

It hadn't helped Arthur much in the Border Sea, because the Mariner had taken so long to come to help. But he *had* come, in the end. The medallion represented a very slim hope for some outside intervention.

Leaf lay in the bed and watched the sleepers pass.

Under the blanket, she tensed and released the muscles in her legs and arms, trying to exercise them back up to speed, to remove the weakness brought on by a week's bed rest.

Finally, after what seemed like a very long time in which several thousand sleepers had passed, she saw the end of the line. Four Denizens followed the last of the humans. They were not quite as splendid as the two who'd preceded Lady Friday, but they were certainly superior Denizens who were intent on doing their job. They stopped by the door and waited, watching the sleeping patients in the beds around Leaf.

Nothing happened for a moment, then the room was suddenly suffused with a soft, golden light, as if a warm summer's afternoon sun had been let in. It disappeared almost as quickly as it came, ebbing back through the far door.

With the retreating light came a summons, direct into Leaf's mind.

"Follow!"

The voice was soft, but it resonated inside Leaf's head, as if she had spoken the word herself while blocking her ears.

The girl felt that single word pull at her, but she was able to resist it. The sleepers felt it more intensely. All around the room, the old folks suddenly sat up, climbed out of bed, and joined the last of the sleepwalkers who were passing through the door.

Leaf got up too and went after them, doing her best impersonation of a sleepwalker, with the final six sleepers and the Denizen rearguard right on her heels. Behind her slack-jawed face, her mind was working furiously, concentrating on repressing the terrible sick feeling of fear and panic that was welling up through her whole body.

Not fear for herself, but for her helpless aunt Mango.

The doors at the far end were open, but Leaf didn't dare to look up and ahead until she was shuffling through the doorway and could pretend to stumble a little in her sleep. The stumble almost turned into a real fall, but her legs were getting stronger with every step, and she managed to stay upright and take a look.

What she saw almost made her stop and give herself away. The large space ahead housed an Olympic-size swimming pool. The pool, however, didn't have any water in it. Instead, a ramp had been built down to the bottom, and right now the last of the sleepwalkers were shambling down it. Down into a mirrored surface, which at first reflected their approach, and then just . . . swallowed them whole.

Leaf hesitated again at the top of the ramp. There were those four Denizens behind her, but there were also several other doors out of the pool room. If she ran now, she might be able to get through one of the exits. It might be her only chance of escape.

But her aunt had already gone beyond the mirrored bottom of the dry pool. . . .

Leaf took a step forward and then another, looking through slitted eyes. She saw the fear in her face, staring back up as her feet disappeared from view. She could still feel her limbs, the sensation being transmitted up through her legs indicating that she was walking down a gentle slope. Leaf suddenly felt physically ill, just like when she'd been vomiting out the mold. Desperate not to throw up, she shut her eyes and plunged forward, her arms outstretched in front, as she committed herself to whatever lay beyond the reflection of Lady Friday's sleepers.

If there *was* anything beyond. . . .

Chapter One

The Nithling soldier thrust its crackling, electrically charged spear towards Arthur's chest. At the very last moment, just as he was about to be impaled, he managed to block the thrust with his shield, the spear point scratching up and across with a horrifying shriek of metal on metal. Arthur stabbed back with his savage-sword, but the Nithling dodged aside and then leaped upon him, knocking him down as its taloned fingers ripped at his face —

Arthur sat up in bed, screaming, his hands scrabbling for a weapon. His fingers closed on a sword hilt and he picked it up and hacked at his attacker — who melted into thin air as he became fully awake. The sword in his hand transformed itself, changing from a slim rapier to a marshal's gold-wreathed ivory baton, the shape the Fourth Key appeared to prefer when Arthur was carrying it.

Arthur put the baton down and took a deep breath. His heart was still hammering as if a crazed blacksmith were at work in his chest, the fear from his nightmare only slowly fading.

Not that the waking world was all that much better. Arthur looked hopefully at the silver crocodile ring on his finger, the one that indicated just how much sorcery had seeped into his blood and bone. But it was no different than it had been the night before. Five of the ten marked segments of the ring had turned gold, indicating he was now at least half Denizen. Every time Arthur used a Key or some other sorcery he would be affected, and the ring would measure the contamination. If the gold spread across just one more segment, the process would be irreversible and he would never be able to return home. Not without negatively affecting everyone and everything he loved. Denizens had a bad effect on life in the Secondary Realms.

"Home!" said Arthur. He was really awake now and every one of his many problems clamored in his head, demanding he think about them. But foremost of them all was his desire to find out what was going on back home and to check that everyone was all right.

He slid out from under the heavy satin sheets and off the feather-stuffed mattress on its four-poster base of mahogany. Each of the posts was carved with battle scenes, which distracted him for a moment, so he found out the hard way that it was farther to the ground than he expected.

He was just getting up off the floor when a discreet knock came at the door.

"Come in!" Arthur called out as he looked around. He'd been so exhausted battling to defend the Citadel against the New Nithling army that he'd hardly noticed where they'd carried him off to sleep. Clearly it was the bedroom of some very superior officer — probably Sir Thursday himself — for as well as the ornate bed there were several gilded, overstuffed armchairs; a richly woven carpet that depicted yet another battle scene, this one a vast spray of orange-red firewash over a horde of misshapen old-style Nithlings; a washstand with a solid gold washbasin and several thick fluffy towels; and an open door leading to a walk-in wardrobe absolutely stuffed full of different uniforms, boots, and accoutrements.

"Good morning, Lord Arthur. Are you ready to be shaved?"

The Denizen who came in was a Corporal wearing the scarlet tunic and black trousers of the Regiment, but he also had a white apron over his tunic, and what appeared to be a brass bowl on his head. He carried a leather case, which he deftly laid on the side table and opened to reveal several brushes and a number of very sharp-looking cutthroat razors.

"Uh, yes, but with the back of the blade, please," said Arthur, without really thinking. He'd gotten used to "shaving" during his recruit training, even though at age twelve he had no whiskers to come off and wouldn't need to shave for a couple of years.

The Corporal gestured to Arthur to sit, took the bowl off his head, filled it with water from the washstand's elephant trunk spout, and began to whisk up a lather.

Arthur sat down, then stood straight back up. "I haven't got time for this!" he said hurriedly. "I have to find out what's going on."

"And so you shall, sir," said a new voice from the door. It was Marshal Dusk, looking much cleaner and tidier in his dark gray uniform than when Arthur had last seen him in the aftermath of battle. "It was Thursday's custom to hear the morning news as he was shaved and dressed. Would you care to follow this practice?"

Arthur looked down at himself. He hadn't realized he was wearing pajamas. Regimental pajamas of scarlet and gold, complete with fringed gold epaulettes that irritated his neck. He was sure they would have woken him if he hadn't been too tired to notice.

"I guess I do have to get dressed. . . ."

He sat back down and the barber instantly applied lather to his cheeks and chin. Dusk marched into the room and stood at attention opposite, while another Corporal, in a more usual cap, came in and marched past into the wardrobe.

"What are the new Nithlings doing? Has the Piper been seen?" asked Arthur. He tried not to move his mouth too much when he talked. The barber was using the back of the razor to just scrape the lather off, but it still made Arthur nervous.

The new Nithlings who served the Piper, the enigmatic second son of the Architect and the Old One, had almost won the battle against Arthur and the Army of the House the night before, coming frighteningly close to capturing the Citadel. Only the arrival of Dame Primus wielding the first Three Keys, accompanied by a large force drawn from the Lower House, the Far Reaches, and the Border Sea, had saved the day.

Arthur had to admit the treachery of the Fourth Part of the Will had also played an important part. In its snake form, it had spat acid in the Piper's mask while he was supposed to be negotiating with Arthur. The absence of the Piper — and whatever powers he possessed, which were likely to be considerable — had quite possibly made the difference between victory and defeat. Not that Arthur approved of the Will's treachery.

"The New Nithlings have remained within their trench

lines overnight, opposite the Citadel," reported Marshal Dusk. "Our troops elsewhere in the Great Maze also report no offensive activity. But the situation is still very serious. There are close to a million enemy soldiers in the Great Maze and we do not know what the Piper is up to or where he is."

"Where's Dame Primus?" Arthur asked as his face was wiped with a hot towel. He had no idea how the barber had made it hot — it just was. "And is there any word of my friends Suzy Turquoise Blue and Fred Gold?"

"Dame Primus awaits you in the operations room," Dusk replied. "I'm afraid we have no news of the captured Piper's children. A detachment of Scouts has been ordered to investigate tile 500/500, where the Nothing Spike was. It's possible they may have something to report later today, via a communications figure."

"Thanks." Arthur stood up as the barber finished and packed away his things, then mechanically returned his salute. The other Corporal came out with a selection of uniforms and laid them on the end of the bed. Then he went in and got some more while Arthur was staring at them, his mind elsewhere. He was thinking about Suzy and Fred, and Leaf back on Earth, and his family. There were so many people he had to think about, so many enemies and troubles, not to mention the fate of the entire universe. . . .

"Which uniform do you require today, sir?" asked the Corporal. "I have suitably enhanced uniforms based upon those for a General of the Regiment, a Khanmander of the Horde, a Legate of the Legion —"

"I'll do the same as Sir Thursday," said Arthur. "Regimental Private, with the appropriate rank badges."

The Corporal suppressed a sigh and returned to the wardrobe, emerging seconds later with the requested clothing. He tried to help Arthur put it on, with little success, as Arthur quickly dressed himself.

Conspicuously, neither the Corporal nor Dusk attempted to hand Arthur the Fourth Key. Now that Arthur had claimed it, it might well incinerate or otherwise destroy anyone else who picked it up. He handled it quite reluctantly himself, for he knew well the temptation to use the power of the Keys to the Kingdom . . . even if it meant he became less human, less himself.

Arthur hesitated, then thrust the baton through the loop on his belt and made sure it was secure. He didn't want to use the Fourth Key, but there was some comfort in its weight at his hip. Just threatening to use it might well be a great help in some situations.

"To the operations room, Lord Arthur?" asked Marshal Dusk, breaking in on Arthur's not-too-cheerful thoughts. "Dame Primus awaits you."

"Yes," said Arthur. He always had a slight, nagging suspicion that Dame Primus, if left to her own devices, would pursue things that might not be in Arthur's best interests. She could only be worse with the addition of Part Four of the Will, the treacherous and highly judgmental snake.

It turned out that the bedroom was in one of the upper levels of the Star Fort, so it was not far to go to the operations room. Arthur was a little surprised to see a whole lot of guards waiting outside his bedroom. There were eight Legionaries in full armor with shields and savage-swords who marched in front of him and eight Borderers with muscle-fiber longbows who fell in behind him as he moved along the corridor from the bedroom. He supposed it was sensible, given that at any moment the Piper could use the Improbable Stair, or perhaps other means, to appear anywhere in the House or the Secondary Realms.

Thinking of the Stair and the guards reminded Arthur about Sir Thursday, who he hoped was still locked up, secure both from escape and from outside attackers. The three previous Trustees that Arthur had deposed had all been killed, probably because they knew something that would be helpful to Arthur and the Will.

"Is Sir Thursday safe?" Arthur asked.

"He is imprisoned and watched," Dusk reported. "Dame Primus spoke to him in the night, but otherwise he has been held incommunicado. The guards know to look out for assassins or raids."

"Good." Arthur was about to ask something else, but before he could, the guards in front flung the door to the operations room open and a Sergeant-Major inside shouted, "Stand fast! Sir Arthur!"

Arthur entered the large, domed chamber as everyone inside — except Dame Primus — snapped to attention. The room looked much as it had the night before, but this time Arthur had a little more time to take in the details, since he wasn't being viciously attacked by Sir Thursday.

The first thing he noticed, behind a solid line of officers and a few Sergeants, all still at attention, was a large square table with Dame Primus looming over it at the far end. Arthur marched towards her, then as everyone was still standing at attention, he remembered to say, "As you were, please. Carry on."

Officers and NCOs — Sergeants and Corporals — began to bustle around and talk again, keeping their voices low, making a steady hum in the background that made the room sound as if it were inhabited by a host of bees. Dame Primus, who was now close to eight feet tall and resplendent in a long scarlet-and-gold robe, inclined her head slightly to Arthur as he approached. He nodded back, noting that while she wore the very fancy robe it was brought in at the waist by a plain, though highly polished, leather belt. The belt supported the clock-hand sword that was the First Key, the pair of folded gauntlets that were the Second Key, and, in a special scabbard on her left hip, the small trident that was the Third Key.

Arthur felt a peculiar pang as he saw the Keys, a desire to take them back from Dame Primus. At the same time, the baton of the Fourth Key shifted on his belt, as if it too was drawn to the other Keys.

To combat the feeling, which he didn't like, Arthur looked away, down at the tabletop. At first sight, it appeared to be just a boring grid of extremely small squares, with no detail whatsoever. But after a second, he suddenly felt as if he were falling into the grid. Details zoomed towards him. The squares got bigger and showed the terrain in them, and then as the zooming sensation continued, he saw tiny models representing House troops and New Nithling soldiers, many surmounted by a code like *2 hrs ago* or a simple question mark.

Arthur blinked, fought back a dizzy feeling, swallowed the faint trace of bile that had risen in his mouth, and the map was just a grid again.

"The map table shows the disposition of our forces and confirmed sighting reports of the enemy," explained Dusk as Arthur rubbed his eyes. "It takes some practice to use it effectively, since it can make new viewers ill."

"There are plenty of practiced map viewers here, Lord Arthur," Dame Primus interjected. She clicked her fingers and a very thick, hardbound book fell out of thin air and landed on her hand. It was heavy enough to break the fingers of a mortal, but she caught it easily. It looked a bit familiar to Arthur, and he soon found out why. "You need not look at the map yourself. Now that you are here, we can get on with important matters of high strategy. I have organized the agenda —"

Arthur held up his hand. "Not the agenda again, please. First of all, I need to know what has happened back home. Is Leaf all right? And what did happen with the Skinless Boy? Is he . . . it . . . totally destroyed?"

Dame Primus sniffed in annoyance and dropped the agenda book. It was caught with two hands by a Corporal who dived in from behind her, the lesser Denizen grunting with the effort.

"There are more pressing matters, Lord Arthur. We are

at war with the Piper and his New Nithlings, you know. Not to mention the remaining Morrow Days."

"I do know," said Arthur grimly. "Where are Dr. Scamandros and Sunscorch?"

"All Denizens not directly required here have reported back to their proper posts," said Dame Primus. "As I am here with three Keys and yourself with another, we do not need excessive Denizen-power and there are many other demands upon our resources."

"I wanted to talk to Dr. Scamandros in particular," said Arthur. He was vaguely troubled by the absence of Scamandros and Sunscorch, who were friends as well as important allies. Even more important, Dr. Scamandros was an Upper House–trained sorcerer, the only one who did not serve Superior Saturday.

"I have sent Dr. Scamandros to the Lower House to keep an eye on the Old One, among other things," said Dame Primus. "There have been some strange occurrences in the Lower Coal Cellar."

"What about Monday's Noon and Dusk?" asked Arthur. "Have they gone back to the Lower House too?"

Dame Primus nodded and looked down at Arthur, arching her long fingers together and looking at him over her sharp nails in a rather unnerving manner.

"There is trouble in every demesne of the House, Lord

Arthur. Nithlings of the old-fashioned sort are bubbling out of every crack and crevice in the Lower House. Our efforts to fill in the Pit in the Far Reaches have met with setbacks and there is considerable danger that some parts of it may fall into the void.

"I have not had time to force the Border Sea within its bounds, and Nothing is leaking into the Sea in many places. Needless to say, our efforts to rectify the situation are being thwarted at every turn by the faithless Trustees, notably Superior Saturday. Now we have the Piper in league with them as well."

"I don't think he's in league with the Trustees," said Arthur. "He thinks he should be the Rightful Heir, not me. He's as much their enemy as I am."

"Perhaps," said Dame Primus in a doubting tone. "In any case, in due course he will be brought to judgment. What we must decide now —"

"I want to know what's happened to Leaf and my family!" interrupted Arthur. "Then as soon as I can, I want to go home. Even if Mom and Dad don't know I've been gone, I miss them! I miss everyone! And before you get started, I know I can't stay. I'll be back to go get the Fifth Key from Lady Friday and do whatever else has to be done, but I . . . I absolutely have to go home for a visit first."

"That is not possible at the moment," said Dame

Primus airily. "As of dawn this morning, Superior Saturday has shut down all the elevators in the demesnes of the House that we control, and she has ordered the Front Door shut to us."

"What? How can she do that?"

"She has the authority," said Dame Primus. "Unless Lord Sunday countermands her orders, Superior Saturday controls much of the interdemesne operations of the House — including elevators and, to some extent, the Front Door. She has also attempted to shut down the telephones, without complete success, as the operators fall under the authority of the Lower House and the metaphysical wiring under the Far Reaches."

"I could go home by the Improbable Stair," said Arthur slowly. He was unable to stop himself from looking at the ring on his finger. He would have to use the power of the Fourth Key to walk the Stair — and every step he took along that strange way would take him farther away from humanity, even as he walked towards his home.

"I would strongly advise against that," said Dame Primus. "You have been very fortunate to survive two perambulations on the Improbable Stair. Now let us move on to the agen —"

"Where's Captain Drury?" interrupted Arthur. He looked away from Dame Primus and saw the telephone expert already hurrying across the room. As he approached, Drury took the old-fashioned handset out of the wicker-work suitcase that housed the body of the field telephone. The captain handed this to Arthur and started to wind the crank, as the boy said, "Get me Sneezer, in the Lower House, please, Captain."

"As you are too busy to discuss strategic plans, Lord Arthur, I shall go interrogate the Piper's children," said Dame Primus, with a very haughty sniff.

"What?" asked Arthur, lowering the handset. "*Which* Piper's children?"

"The ones that are serving here in the Citadel," said Dame Primus. "The Piper has declared himself our enemy. The children were originally brought to the House by him, for his own purposes. Therefore they are now enemies too and must be judged accordingly."

As she spoke, Dame Primus's tongue briefly forked and turned a sickly green, and her two eyeteeth grew long and pointed, exactly like the fangs of the snake-form that Part Four of the Will had taken.

Arthur stepped back and his hand instinctively went to the Fourth Key on his belt.

Dame Primus frowned and took a dainty lace handker-chief out of her sleeve and dabbed at her mouth. When she lowered the handkerchief, the forked tongue and fangs had vanished. She was once more just a very beautiful but stern-looking eight-foot-tall woman.

"Do not be alarmed, Arthur. We are still assimilating the most recent part of our self, and it is inclined to be judgmental. Now, where was I? Oh yes, Piper's children. I expect that after a quick trial we shall have no choice."

Without a moment's hesitation, Dame Primus proclaimed, "Here and everywhere else in the House where we hold sway, all Piper's children must be executed!"

Chapter Two

Arthur hung up the phone and looked at Dame Primus.

"No Piper's children are going to be executed," he said firmly. "Here or anywhere else. The only time the Piper controlled any of them is when he was close enough for his pipe-playing to be heard. Even then, all that happened was they just stopped moving."

"He could undoubtedly do much more," Dame Primus argued. "Perhaps even from outside the House. We do not know the extent of his powers. It would be best to simply get rid of the Piper's children."

"No!" shouted Arthur. "What's wrong with you? They're people! You can't just kill hundreds or thousands of Piper's children because the Piper might . . . just *might* . . . make some of them do something."

"Can't we?" asked Dame Primus. She sounded genuinely puzzled.

"No," said Arthur. His voice grew deeper and stronger. "All Piper's children are to be released unharmed and restored to their normal jobs and positions. They should be watched, and if . . . *if* they do something against us, that's when they should be locked up — and only locked up, nothing worse!"

There was a moment's silence, even the background buzz of talking soldiers absent. Dame Primus inclined her head a fraction of an inch.

"Very well, Lord Arthur. You are the Rightful Heir. It shall be as you wish."

"Good," said Arthur. "Now I'm going to call Sneezer and get him to find out what is happening back home."

He took the phone again from Captain Drury, who resumed his cranking. The earpiece crackled and hummed, and in the far distance Arthur could hear a stern male voice saying, "All telephones are to be cut off by order," but that faded as another, softer voice that might be either male or female said, "Shut up."

"I beg your pardon?" asked Arthur.

"Not you, sorry," said the voice. "Can I help you?"

"I'd like to speak to Sneezer in Monday's Dayroom, please."

"Ooh, you're Lord Arthur, aren't you? I could tell because you said 'please' again. Everyone's saying how nice you are."

"Uh, thanks," said Arthur. "Could I speak to Sneezer? It really is urgent."

"Putting you through, Lord Arthur," said the operator. "Even if old grizzleguts says we're . . ."

The operator's voice faded and Arthur heard a multitude of other, distant voices all speaking at once, overlaid with the stern voice once again ordering that all telephones be cut off. Then there was silence for several seconds. Arthur was about to ask Captain Drury what was going on when the familiar voice of Sneezer sounded out in the air, not out of the phone.

"Monday's Dayroom, Sneezer here."

"It does that sometimes, sir," whispered Drury.

"It's Arthur, Sneezer."

"Good day to you, Lord Arthur."

"Sneezer, I want you to look through the Seven Dials. I need to find out what's happened to Leaf and my family, and the general situation back at my home. Can you do that, please?"

"I can, sir. Indeed, at the behest of Dr. Scamandros I have already looked through, the doctor being desirous of finding out if any Nothing residue of the Skinless Boy remained."

"What did you see?" asked Arthur. "It's still Thursday there, right?"

"No, Lord Arthur. It is Friday."

"Friday! If the Skinless Boy was destroyed on

Thursday . . . I'll have been missing overnight. My parents must be freaking out!"

"To be exact, Friday a week from the Thursday on which Miss Leaf embarked on her action against the Skinless Boy."

"A week! You mean I've been missing on Earth for a week?!"

"I believe that is so, sir. Dr. Scamandros has suggested that the destruction of the Skinless Boy created a minor fracture of the temporal relationship between you and the Secondary Realm in which you normally reside."

"My parents must think . . . What's happened to my mom and dad?"

"I regret to inform you, Lord Arthur, that while your father is safe — though reluctantly engaged in being driven very long distances in a bus and stopping at night to play music with an ensemble named after rodents — it appears that your mother is not currently in your own Secondary Realm —"

"What?" croaked Arthur. His throat felt suddenly choked and dry. "Where is she? Who . . . how . . ."

"There is great disturbance in your world, Lord Arthur," said Sneezer. His voice was getting fainter. "A number of mortals have been taken elsewhere within the

Secondary Realms. I think your mother is among that group, though it is possible that not all the disappearances have been effectuated by the same agency. It is not at all clear who is responsible, though the natural assumption would be Lady Friday, since the disappearances appear to have occurred on that day."

Arthur forced himself to be calm, to try to think, not just panic. But the panic was bubbling up inside him. He wanted to just shut his eyes and fade out until someone else took care of everything. But someone else wasn't going to take care of him, or his mother, or anything. . . .

He took two breaths that were not as deep as he wanted them to be, though it was shock and fear affecting his lungs, not his usual asthma. He didn't suffer from asthma in the House.

"Find out where Mom is . . . where they all are," he ordered Sneezer. "Get Dr. Scamandros on it. Get anyone who can help to . . . to help. Oh — what about Leaf? Is she okay?"

"I believe Miss Leaf is one of the abducted mortals," said Sneezer carefully. His voice was very faint now, as if the telephone was a long way from his mouth. "One of the main group of abductees, that is to say. Though in her case she might have chosen to go along. I couldn't get a clear view of the proceedings; there was an opacity resulting from some opposing power. However, it appeared —"

"Get off!" said the operator suddenly, over the top of Sneezer's voice. "No, I'm not coming down the line. . . . Get off! Stop it! Ah! Help! It's got my foot — pull me back, lads! Heave!"

A whole host of voices joined in then, shouting and screaming, and whatever Sneezer was saying was lost. Then there was a deafening howl, as if someone had trod on the tail of an extremely large and unfriendly wolf, and the handset crumbled into dust in Arthur's hands, leaving him holding a single wire that let out a small and pathetic spark before he hastily dropped it.

"We have to find my mom," said Arthur.

"Your destiny does not include a mortal family," Dame Primus declared. "As I have said before, you should shake off those minor shackles. As I understand it, your parents are not blood relations, in any case."

"They're my parents," Arthur protested. He had long since gotten used to being adopted, but there was still some sting in the Will's words. "Emily and Bob love me, and I love them. I love all my family."

"That is a mortal invention," said Dame Primus. "It is of no use in the House."

"What?" asked Arthur.

"Love," Dame Primus answered, her lips twisted in distaste. "Now, Lord Arthur, I really *must* insist that we attend to at least the most significant items of the agenda. I have reordered it as you requested."

"I requested?" Arthur's voice was vacant, since he was still in shock. He'd tried so hard to protect his family. Everything he'd done had been to keep them out of things. But it hadn't worked. Superior Saturday had threatened to use the Skinless Boy to take his place, to erase their minds so they forgot the real Arthur. Since that hadn't worked, maybe now Friday or Saturday had kidnapped his mom. . . . Arthur's mind raced as he tried to get a grip on the situation.

"At our meeting in Monday's Dayroom," said Dame Primus. "Before you were drafted. Do pay attention, Lord Arthur."

"I'm thinking," snapped Arthur. "Captain Drury, do you have a spare phone? I have to get Sneezer on the line again. And Dr. Scamandros."

"Arthur, this is not —"

Dame Primus got no further, as two of Arthur's Legionary guards suddenly grabbed him and pulled him back, and two more jumped in front of him and locked their shields with an almighty crash. The embodiment of the Will leaped back too, and all over the room there was the sudden whine of savage-swords and the acrid, ozone smell of lightning-charged tulwars as everyone drew their weapons.

Arthur couldn't even see what his guards had reacted to, until he stood on tiptoe and looked over the locked shields to see that someone had appeared only a few feet in front of where he'd been standing.

That someone was a tall, slight female Denizen clad in a very unmilitary flowing robe made of thousands of tiny silver strips that chinked as she moved. Over that beautiful garment she wore a thick leather apron, with several pockets out of which protruded the wooden handles of weapons or perhaps tools. This strange ensemble was completed by the silver branch she held in her right hand, from which a dozen small cylindrical fruits of spun gold hung suspended, tinkling madly as half a dozen Denizens threw themselves upon her.

"I'm a messenger!" she shouted. "A herald! Not an assassin! Look, I've got an olive branch!"

"Looks more like a lemon branch," said the Legionary Decurion as he twisted it out of the Denizen's grasp. He looked over at Arthur. "Sorry, sir! We'll have her out of here in a moment!"

"I'm an emissary from Lady Friday!" shouted the silver-robed Denizen, who could hardly be seen amid the scrum of soldiers. "I insist on an audience with Lord Arthur!"

"Wait!" Arthur and Dame Primus called out at the same time.

The Legionaries stopped dragging the sudden visitor away, though they kept a very firm grip on her.

"Who are you?" demanded Dame Primus at the same time that Arthur asked, "How did you get here?"

"I'm Emelena Folio Gatherer, Second Grade, 10,218th in precedence within the House," declared the Denizen. "I have been sent as a herald to Lord Arthur, with a message from Lady Friday, who sent me here through her mirror."

"Through her mirror?" asked Arthur, as Dame Primus said, "What message?"

Arthur and Dame Primus looked at each other for a long moment. Finally the embodiment of the Will lowered her chin very slightly. Arthur turned back to Emelena.

"What mirror?"

"Lady Friday's mirror," said Emelena. She added hesitantly, "Am I correct in assuming that I address Lord Arthur?"

"Yes, I'm Arthur."

Emelena mumbled something that Arthur correctly

thought was about expecting him to be taller, more impressive, have lightning bolts coming out of his eyes, and so on. Ever since someone in the House had written a book about Lord Arthur, every Denizen he'd met had been disappointed by his lack of heroic stature and presence.

"Lady Friday's mirror," asked Arthur. "It can send you anywhere within the House and the Secondary Realms?"

"I don't know, Lord Arthur," replied Emelena. "I've never been sent anywhere before. Usually I'm a senior page collator of the Guild of Binding and Restoration in the Middle House."

"Friday's mirror is known to us, Lord Arthur," said Dame Primus through pursed lips. She looked around the room, then pointed to a highly polished metal shield that was one of the trophies hung on the wall. "Someone take that shield down and put it in the dark."

She paused to watch several Denizens dash forward to carry out her orders, then continued, "Friday's mirror is akin to the Seven Dials in the Lower House. Powered by the Fifth Key, she can look out or send Denizens through any mirror or reflective surface, provided she has been there before herself by more usual means. Which does make us wonder when and why Lady Friday has come here before to meet with Sir Thursday. However, what is of most importance now is the message Lady Friday sends. I trust it is her unconditional and total surrender?"

"After a fashion," said Emelena. "I think. Perhaps."

This time, Arthur was silent, while Dame Primus drew in her breath with an all-too-snakelike hiss.

"Shall I tell you the message?" asked Emelena. "I've got it memorized."

"Go ahead," said Arthur.

Emelena took a deep breath, clasped her hands together, and without looking directly at Arthur or Dame Primus, began to speak a little too fast and without emphasizing the punctuation, though she did stop every now and then to draw breath.

greetings lord arthur from lady friday trustee of the architect and mistress of the middle house i greet you through my mouthpiece who is to deliver my words exactly as i have spoken them knowing full well that you seek the fifth key and will stop at nothing to get it as saturday and the piper will likewise do

and in the interest of a quiet life pursuing my own researches into aspects of mortality i have decided to abdicate as mistress of the fifth house and leave the key for whomsoever might find it and wield it as he or she sees fit

i ask only that i be left alone in my sanctuary which lies outside the house in the secondary realms with such servants as who choose to join me there my messengers have gone to saturday and the piper bearing this same offer

whoever of you three can find and take the key from where it lies within my scriptorium in the middle house is welcome to it the key shall accept you or saturday or the piper the fifth part of the Will I also leave in the middle house and I take no further responsibility for its incarceration but shall not release it either lest it take the Key itself

my abdication shall take place upon the moment all three of you have read this message and at that moment this act shall be recorded on the metal tablet my messenger also bears

Emelena stopped, took a deep breath, and bowed. When she stood up, she added, "I have the metal tablet in an envelope here, Lord Arthur."

She took a small but heavy buff-colored envelope out of her apron pocket and held it out to Arthur. He instinctively reached for it and his fingers had just touched the envelope when Dame Primus shouted, "No! Don't take —"

Her warning came a fraction of a second too late, as Arthur's fingers closed and Emelena's let go. As he took the weight, Arthur felt a sudden surge of sorcerous energy erupt out of the package. The envelope blew apart in a shower of tiny confetti and Arthur had a fraction of a second to see that what he was now holding was a small round plate made of some highly burnished silvery metal.

Then everything around him vanished, to be replaced by a sudden rush of freezing air, the nauseous shock of disorientation, and the sudden fearful realization that he was falling . . . followed seconds later by his sudden impact with the ground.

Chapter Three

Arthur lay stunned for several seconds. He wasn't hurt, but was seriously shocked from the sudden shift from where he'd been to where he was now, which was flat on his back in a deep drift of snow. Looking up, all he could see were large, puffy gray clouds and some lazy, downward-spiraling snowflakes. One landed in his open mouth, prompting him to shut it.

The silvery disk of metal from Lady Friday was still in his hand. Arthur raised his head a little and looked at it. He'd never seen the metal electrum before, but this plate was certainly made of that alloy of silver and gold, which he'd learned was the traditional material of Transfer Plates. Like the one he was holding in his hand. It must have been set to transfer whoever took it from the messenger, as soon as he or she touched it.

In other words, it was a trap that had instantly transported Arthur from the relative safety of the Great Maze to somewhere else. Somewhere where he would be more vulnerable. . . .

Arthur's thinking suddenly became more organized,

the momentary shock of the transfer banished by sudden adrenaline. He sat up and took a careful look around, at the same time taking a series of deep breaths. The look was to see if there were any immediate enemies approaching. The deep breaths were to see if his asthma was coming back. If it was, then that would mean he had left the House and was somewhere on Earth . . . or some other Secondary Realm.

His breathing was easy, unaffected by the shock and cold. Still, Arthur was puzzled. It didn't look like any part of the House that he knew. It was too naturalistic. Usually you could tell that the sky was in fact a ceiling way above, or the sun moved in a jerky, clockwork way. Here, everything felt like it would back on Earth.

It was certainly cold and he was very wet from the snow. Arthur shivered and then shivered again. It took concentrated effort not to keep on shivering. To take his mind off it, he stood up and vigorously brushed off the snow. Not that it did much good, since the drift came up to his thighs.

"I wonder if I can freeze to death?" Arthur said aloud. Though he spoke softly, it was so quiet around him that even his own voice was a bit disturbing. So was the question. He knew that he couldn't die of hunger or thirst in the House, and that the Fourth Key would to some degree protect him from physical threats, though not from pain and suffering. But he was still mortal and he was feeling very cold indeed.

Thinking of the Fourth Key made Arthur slap his side in a sudden panic, the panic immediately replaced with relief as his hand touched the baton. It hadn't fallen out, which was a very good thing, since he'd never be able to find it under all the snow.

It also made him feel better to know that even if he had been transported into a trap, he had a weapon. Not that he planned to use the sorcerous powers of the Key, but the baton could turn into a sword and he could certainly use that, after all his training at Fort Transformation and the battle with the New Nithlings.

Arthur frowned. He hadn't wanted to remember the battle. It was bad enough having nightmares about it, without having sudden flashes of memory from that fight forcing everything else out of his head. He didn't want to relive the sights and sounds and emotions of that day.

He shivered again, as much at the memory as from the cold. He looked around again. He had to find shelter, and quickly, and there was no obvious direction to walk in. Or *wade* in, since the snow was so deep.

"That's as good as any," said Arthur to himself as he looked towards where he thought the snow and low cloud cover were a little clearer than elsewhere. He tucked the transfer plate inside his coat, took four clumsy steps, then stopped and stood completely still, his heart racing.

There were dark shapes emerging out of the snow some fifty yards ahead, at the limit of visibility. Familiar, but totally unwelcome shapes. Man-sized, wearing dark, very old-fashioned suits, topped with bowler hats. Arthur couldn't see their faces, but he knew they'd be as ugly and bejowled as a bloodhound's — the dog-faces of Nithling servants.

"Fetchers!" whispered Arthur; without conscious thought, the Fourth Key was in his hand, an ivory baton stretching out as it transformed into a silver-bladed rapier.

There were six of the Nithlings in sight. They hadn't seen Arthur yet, or smelled him, since there was no wind. He watched them, weighing his plan of attack. If he moved against the two on the right, he could probably get them both before the others reacted. It would only take the slightest touch from the Key to banish them back to Nothing, and then he could charge the next one along. . . .

More Fetchers came into sight behind the first six. A long line of Fetchers, at least fifty of them. Arthur lowered his sword and looked behind him, checking his line of retreat. There were too many Fetchers. He might destroy a dozen and the rest would still pull him down. The Key might do something to protect him then, or he could use its full power to blast the Nithlings from a distance, but that was an absolute last resort. Arthur's humanity was almost as precious to him as his life. If he became a Denizen there would be no hope of any return to his family . . . if he had a family to return to. . . .

Arthur quelled these dismal thoughts and quickly stamped through the snow, away from the Fetchers. At least they were walking slowly, more impeded by the snow than he was, their squat, lumpy bodies sinking farther into the drifts.

They were also looking for something, Arthur saw when he paused to glance back. The first lot of six were an advance guard, but the line behind was a search party, with the Fetchers looking down and even rummaging in the snow every now and then.

Arthur didn't look back again for quite a while, instead concentrating on making good speed. He was becoming quite alarmed at the complete lack of any trees, plants, or buildings — anything that might give him some shelter. As far as he could tell, he was on an endless, snow-swept plain.

He kept going, though, since there didn't seem to be any alternative. After what might have been an hour or more, he was finally rewarded with the glimpse of something up ahead that could only be a building. He only saw it for a second before the snow and clouds swirled around and obscured it again, but it lent him hope. Arthur began to half-run, half-jump towards it.

He got another look a few yards on and instinctively slowed again to take in what he was looking at.

It was a building, he could see that, but a strange one. Through the bands of falling snow he could make out a rectangular outline that looked normal enough — a tower or something similar, perhaps nine or ten floors high, of similar dimensions to a medium-rise office block. But behind that there was something even bigger . . . and that something was moving.

Arthur brushed a snowflake out of his left eye, blinked away the moisture, and marched forward, still intent on the building. He quickly saw that the moving thing was a giant wheel, at least a hundred and forty feet in diameter and perhaps twenty feet wide. It looked quite a lot like a Ferris wheel at an amusement park, though it was made of wood and didn't have little cabins for people to ride in. Its central axle was set about two-thirds of the way up the tower, which was built of dark red brick. Though the lower three floors were solid, above that level it had attractive blue-shuttered windows, all of which were shut.

The wheel was being turned by water. Water poured

down through the slats and spokes as it rotated, and chunks of ice were falling from it too. In addition to the water and ice, there were also other things being lifted up by the wheel on one side, only to fall off on the downward rotation. Arthur had first thought they were larger bits of ice, but as he got closer he saw they were books and stone tablets and bundles of papers tied with ribbon.

He'd seen similar items before, down in the Lower House, and he knew what they had to be. Records. Records of people and life from the Secondary Realms.

The water that drove the wheel, or rather the propelling current, came from a very wide canal, so wide Arthur couldn't see the other side, the water and low cloud cover merging some hundred yards out. A very straight and regular shoreline extended to the left and right of the tower, continuing until it too was lost in cloud and snow in both directions.

Away from the wheel, the edge of the canal was iced over, upthrust fingers of ice holding still more papers, tablets, pieces of beaten bronze, cured sheepskins burnt with symbols, and other unidentifiable objects. Even more documents were bobbing in the open water.

Arthur was more interested in the smoke he noted was rising out of the central stack of six tall chimneys that stood atop the tower. Catching sight of that hint of fire and warmth, he began to progress faster through the snow, jumping when he couldn't physically push through the drifts.

As he drew nearer, Arthur heard the creak and grind of the huge wheel, accompanied by the crunch of breaking ice and the crash of falling water, interspersed with the thud and splash of documents of all kinds falling through the wheel. It was hard to tell what the vast wheel was actually supposed to do. If it was meant to lift the records, then it was failing to do so, since they were falling through the many holes in the slats. The whole thing looked to be in a state of considerable disrepair.

Arthur reached the closest wall, but there was no visible door or other entry point on the side of the tower facing him. He hesitated for a moment, then started to walk around it to the right, choosing that direction at random. He was feeling suddenly more cheerful, with the prospect of shelter close at hand and also somewhere where he would be safe from the Fetchers. Or at least somewhere more defensible, if he had to fight them off.

Then Arthur rounded the corner and he saw two things. The first was a door, as he'd hoped. The second was a group of Fetchers who were sitting or lying in the snow in front of the door, very like a pack of dogs waiting for dinner to be brought out. There were eight of them, and as

Arthur stopped, they all leaped to their feet, jowls wobbling, fierce eyes fixed upon him.

Arthur didn't hesitate. He lunged at the closest Fetcher, even as the others bounded forward. The rapier barely touched it, but the Nithling dissolved into a waft of black smoke and Arthur swung his weapon viciously to the right, the blade sweeping through another two Fetchers as if they were no more solid than the smoke they turned into at the merest touch of the Key. Arthur stamped his foot and advanced on the remaining Nithlings, who growled and circled around to try to get behind him, all of them now intensely wary of his sword. Arthur foiled that by charging up to the wall. Swiveling to place his back against the bricks, he made small thrusts at the Fetchers as they feinted attacks, none of them daring to follow through with a real assault.

Then the biggest, ugliest Fetcher with the least-dented bowler hat spoke, in a voice that was half-growl, half-bark, but clear enough.

"Tell the pack, tell the boss."

A smaller Fetcher turned and darted away, even as Arthur dashed forward and slashed at it and the leader. The small Fetcher was too fast, but the leader paid for its inability to speak and move at the same time, the point of the rapier tearing through the sleeve of its black coat before making coat, hat, and Fetcher disappear in a puff of oily black vapor.

The three remaining Fetchers whimpered and backed away. Arthur let them go, since he hadn't caught the small one anyway. The trio retreated facing him for twenty or thirty yards, then spun about and ran, disappearing into the blur of snow.

A sharp, metallic noise behind and to the left made Arthur himself spin about. The noise came from the door and for a moment he thought it was some weapon being readied behind it. Then he saw there was a metal-lined mail slot in the middle of the door, and the cover of it was flapping.

Arthur pushed the cover open again with the point of his rapier and tried to look inside without getting too close. He was rewarded by the sight of someone recoiling back from the other side, and some muffled sounds that were probably swearing.

"Open up!" commanded Arthur.

Chapter Four

Leaf felt her stomach do a weird flip-flop as she opened her eyes. The line of sleepers still marched on, wandering along a wide corridor roughly hewn out of a dull pink stone, lit every few yards by dragon-headed gas jets of tarnished bronze that spat out long blue flames across the slightly curved ceiling. Leaf tried to keep her place in the line of sleepers, but as she took a step she almost lost her balance, her arms windmilling in a most wide-awake fashion.

For several seconds Leaf staggered forward, trying to regain her balance and act asleep at the same time. It took her several more steps to realize that it wasn't some sort of inner ear problem. Experimenting, she pushed off a little harder — harder than she intended, overcompensating for her bed-weakened legs. She shot up several feet and almost collided with one of the gas jets in the ceiling, even though it was at least nine feet from the floor. Avoiding the flame, she pushed the sleeper ahead of her.

While this confirmed her hypothesis that she was somewhere with lower gravity than Earth, it unfortunately also attracted the attention of the Denizen guards behind her. Two of the final four guards rushed at her, while the others continued on with the few sleepers who were at the end of the line behind her.

Leaf didn't have time to do more than stand up and look back before the duo gripped her arms and hauled her out of the line to stand on one side of the passage. She let her arms go slack, shut her eyes, and let her head hang, as if she had gone back to sleep, but the Denizens weren't fooled this time.

"She's awake," said one. Though she was dressed in the same gray business suit and trench coat as all the others, Leaf could tell from her voice that she was female.

"Maybe," said the other, male Denizen. "What do we do with her if she is?"

"Look it up. Have you got a copy of *Orders and Procedures*?"

"I was working on the binding last night and I put it under a rock to press it, and then I forgot which rock it was under. Can I borrow yours?"

"I've been gilding the initial capitals," answered the female Denizen. "It's on my worktable."

"I suppose we could ask Her. . . ."

Leaf couldn't help but shiver; from the way the Denizen said "Her," it was clear he was talking about Lady Friday.

"Don't be stupid! She doesn't want to be bothered. We had one wake up once before. What did we do with her?"

"I've never had one wake up, Milka."

"It was only twenty years ago, local time. Where were you?"

"Where I wish I still was, Sixth Standby Hand on the Big Press. I only got sent here when Jakem took over the binding line. He never liked me, and all because I accidentally wound one of the lesser presses when his head was in it — and that was more than a thousand years ago —"

"I remember!" said Milka.

"You remember? You weren't there —"

"No, idiot! Not whatever you did. I remember that accidental wake-ups get handed over to the bed turner!"

"Who?"

"The bed turner. You know, the mortal in charge of looking after the sleepers. I forget her name. Or maybe I only knew the name of the one before this one . . . or the one before that. They just don't last long enough to remember."

"Where do we find this bed turner, then?" asked the male Denizen. Leaf decided that she would call him "Stupid" until she heard his actual name. It seemed to be appropriate.

"She's got an office somewhere. Look it up on your

map. You have got your map, haven't you? I'll keep hold of this mortal."

Leaf felt Stupid let go of her and she started to tense her muscles, ready to try to escape if Milka let go as well. But the female Denizen tightened her grip on Leaf's upper arm, her fingers digging in hard.

"No you don't!" said Milka. "I've worked enough with Piper's children to know what you mortals are like. Tricksters, all of you. There's no point in pretending to be asleep. No point running away from us, neither, because there's nowhere to go."

Leaf lifted her head, opened her eyes, and took a long, slow look around. Stupid was clumsily opening up a map that kept on unfolding, growing larger and larger till he had the full eight-by-eight-foot square of thick, linen-rich paper against the wall. Unfortunately, it was the back of the map he was looking at, so he had to turn it over and got rather caught up in it in the process.

Milka sighed, but again did not relax her fierce hold on Leaf's arm.

"What do you mean, there's nowhere to go?" Leaf asked as Stupid continued to struggle with the map. He'd gotten it the right way around but part of it had folded back on itself. From the parts Leaf could see, it looked more like the plan of a building than a map. It was all rooms and corridors, arranged in a large circle around some sort of central lake in the middle. Or something round that was colored blue anyway.

"Oh, given up on the tricksy pretending-to-sleep act, have you?" said Milka. She sounded friendly enough. Or at least not actively hostile. "I meant what I said. This here is Lady Friday's Mountain Retreat. She had the mountain built special back at the House and then shifted it here. That's when the middle bit sank in — it got dropped a bit. Beyond the mountain there's one of the wildest, meanest worlds in all the Secondary Realms. She likes her privacy, she does."

"Found it!" exclaimed Stupid. He put a finger on the map, letting go of one edge in the process. The whole thing collapsed again, folding itself over his head.

"There really is nowhere to run," Milka repeated, with a sharp dig of her fingers. "You just stand against the wall and in a minute we'll take you to the bed turner. Give us trouble and you'll be punished."

She released Leaf and took the map off Stupid, easily refolding it to show the area that he'd indicated earlier.

For a moment Leaf did think of running. But her legs were still weak, her balance was off, and most of all she believed Milka. There probably was nowhere to run to, or at least nowhere immediately obvious. It would be best to go along for now and learn as much as possible about where she was. Then she could work out a plan not just to get away herself but to rescue Aunt Mango — and everyone else, if it was possible.

"Circle Six, Eighteen Past," said Milka. "And we're on Circle Two at Forty-three Past. So we have to go up four circles and either back around or forward. Back would be a bit quicker."

"Why?" asked Stupid.

Milka sighed. "Because counterclockwards around the circle from forty-three to eighteen is twenty-five segments and clockwards from forty-three to eighteen is thirty-five segments."

"Oh, right, I wasn't counting properly," said Stupid. He pointed to his right. "That's forward, isn't it?"

"No, that's backward," said Milka. "You're facing into the crater."

She prodded Leaf. "Come on. The sooner you get delivered, the sooner you get to work."

"Work?" asked Leaf. "What work?"

"You'll find out," said Milka. "Hurry up."

Leaf started walking. Every step felt strange; she had to consciously take smaller, less forceful movements in order to keep her balance. It wasn't like being on the moon — at least she wasn't moving like the Chinese astronauts who'd landed there a few years ago. She guessed it was about eighty-five percent of what was normal on Earth. Enough to upset her balance, that was for sure.

The rough-hewn passage with its gaslights continued for several hundred yards, always curving gently to the left. Every now and then there were doors, sometimes on both sides. Very ordinary-looking wooden doors, all painted pale blue, with a wide variety of bronze knobs and handles that might or might not signify what lay behind them.

"Slow down!" Milka called out. "Take the stairs on the right."

Leaf slowed down. There was an open archway up ahead, on the right. The number 42 was painted in white on the right of the arch — or rather, Leaf saw, the numeral was a mosaic made of small pieces of ivory or something similar. At the apex of the arch there was another white numeral, this time 2.

Through the arch was a landing that had the number 2 inlaid in the floor, again in small white stones or pieces of ivory. From the landing there was a broad stair that went up to the left and down to the right, the steps again carved straight out of the stone, this time faced with a smoother, pale stone with a bluish tint. The stairs were also lit by gas jets, smaller ones than before, which were shaped like crouching leopards and set into the wall rather than the ceiling.

"Up!" ordered Milka.

Leaf turned to the left and started up the steps. She climbed quite a long way before they came to another landing, which had the number 3 on it.

"Three more to go," said Milka.

Even with the lower gravity, it was a long climb. Leaf counted three hundred steps between level three and level four and a similar number between four and five, though she lost count at one point, when her mind was distracted by worries, both for her family and for herself.

They met no one else on the way up and there was no one in evidence when they came out on level 6, or "circle six" as Milka called it. The corridor they entered looked almost exactly like the one the sleepers had taken, way down below, though Leaf did note there was some minor variation in the color and texture of the rock.

"Now we walk around to segment eighteen," said Milka.

"I hate this place," said Stupid. "I wish we were back in the House."

"Quiet!" snapped Milka. "You never know who might hear you!"

"I was just saying —"

"Well, don't. What did I do to get lumbered with you anyway, Feorin?"

Leaf was a bit disappointed to hear Feorin's real name. It made it hard to keep thinking of him as Stupid.

"I don't know," he said now. "Did you accidentally press someone?"

"No. I volunteered. Thought it would lead to promotion. Now be quiet. The sooner we drop off this child, the sooner we can have a cup of tea and put our feet up."

"Tea? Have you got some?" asked Feorin. "Really?"

"Yes. I got a chest from those rats last time we were back home. Hurry up."

They walked considerably faster after the mention of tea, with Feorin leading the way. Judging from the numbers they came across every few hundred yards and from her brief look at the map, Leaf worked out that she was in a circular passage that was divided into chapters — or segments — like a clock. The passage ran along the outer rim of the circle and all the rooms and presumably lesser corridors ran from the rim in towards the center, or at least until they hit whatever the big blue thing was on the map.

Leaf spent some of the time working out how big the circle was. If there were sixty segments and the distance between segments was about three hundred paces, and she knew her paces were about eighteen inches long, then the total circumference was 300 times 1.5 feet, or 450 feet or 150 yards, times 60, which was 9000 yards or about 5 miles. From that, using $c=2\pi r$ she could calculate the diameter. . . .

Leaf was so intent on working this out in her head that she didn't realize that Feorin had suddenly stopped. She ran into his back and bounced off, losing her balance and landing on her bottom.

Leaf started to get up but instantly decided to stay where she was as Feorin threw his arms back, his trench coat flew off, and his eggshell-blue wings exploded out, the trailing feathers brushing across her face. At the same time, he drew a short sword or a long dagger from a sheath at his side, a dagger whose mirrored blade sent bright reflections leaping across the walls.

Milka followed suit a fraction of a second later and actually leaped over Leaf, the gas flame in the ceiling whooshing as she passed through it. Like Feorin, her wings were pale blue, and she too had a mirror-surfaced dagger.

Leaf couldn't see what they were attacking — or defending against — because the Denizens' weapons were too bright. All she saw were the flicker of wings and a blur of light like the photon trails left in long-exposure photographs of nighttime traffic.

Then Feorin was hurled past her, thrown at least thirty

feet back down the passage. He hit the floor and skidded along at least another twenty feet before hitting a curve of the wall.

Leaf saw the attacker then. Or part of it — a long, gray tendril or tentacle as thick as her leg and ten feet long, which was connected to a gray, mottled object the shape of an oval football but as big as a refrigerator. It was scuttling backwards like a huge rat, though she could see no legs. Leaf only got to see it for a second before Milka cut the tendril into several bits and then plunged her dagger into the football-shaped thing with a flash of light so intense that Leaf was not only blinded but felt a heat on her face as if she had been instantly sunburned.

It took several seconds for her vision to come back, seconds spent stunned as her mind and body began to work out that she should actually be seriously afraid and doing something, preferably running away.

But when her sight began to return, complete with floating dots and blotchy bits, Leaf quelled her fear. She was aided in this because Milka was kicking small black-ened fragments of the thing she'd fought into a pile, in a manner that indicated it was no longer any sort of threat. And Feorin was walking back, seemingly unconcerned.

"What was *that*?" asked Leaf. Her voice sounded small and scared and distant, even to herself.

Chapter Five

"Open up!" repeated Arthur. "Or else I'll blast this door off its hinges!"

He withdrew his rapier from the mail slot and it transformed back into a baton. Arthur hoped this meant that no immediate enemies were in the vicinity and that whoever was behind the door was friendly, or at least neutral. He figured he likely had only minutes before a whole lot more Nithlings showed up — probably with their boss. That could be anyone or anything, he guessed, ranging from Saturday's Dusk to one of the Piper's New Nithling officers. Whoever it was, Arthur wanted to be inside the tower before they arrived.

There was no immediate response to his shout. Arthur was just drawing breath to repeat his order for the third time, and wondering what he would actually do if they didn't open up, when he heard the sound of several bolts being withdrawn on the other side of the door, followed by the door itself creaking open.

A thin but very wiry Denizen poked his head around

nervously and said, "Come in, sir, come in. You won't slay us all, will you?"

"I won't slay anyone," said Arthur.

The Denizen stood aside as the boy came through, then pushed the foot-thick iron-bound door closed with considerable effort and slid home several huge bolts, then lowered a bar that looked as if it would be more at home as the central prop for a very deep mine, where it could hold up tons and tons of rock.

Arthur looked around at the small antechamber, but there was nothing of interest to see apart from slightly damp stone walls and another, closed door opposite of a less sturdy appearance. It was still very cold.

"I just want to get warm," said Arthur. "Who are you?"

"Marek Flat Gold, sir. Leading Foilmaker, Second Class, 97,858th in precedence within the House. You're not going to slay us? Or destroy the mill?"

"No," said Arthur. He didn't pause to wonder why a Denizen who towered over him could be so afraid of a young, mortal boy. Marek hesitated, then opened the inner door and gestured for Arthur to go ahead.

The boy walked through, but recoiled as he passed the threshold and felt a wave of heat roll over him, accompanied by fierce yellow light.

"Wow, it's hot in here!"

He felt like he'd walked from the snow into a sauna. Past the door was a huge open area, as big as a sports arena, far larger than was possible from the tower's outer dimensions. Arthur was used to that; in the House many buildings were larger on the inside than they seemed on the outside. What he hadn't been prepared for was the heat, the rich red and yellow light, and the source of both: a huge pool of molten gold in the middle of the chamber. It was as big as an Olympic-size swimming pool, but instead of being sunk into the ground, it was built up, its clear crystal sides at least six feet high.

Red-hot liquid gold flowed from the big pool along an open gutter of crystal that was supported by stilts of dark iron, ending up in a series of six smaller pools. At each of these, Denizens scooped the gold up with tools that looked like big cups on the end of ten-foot-long metal poles. The gold-carriers then took their cups to another corner of the chamber, where it was cast into ingots. The still-hot ingots were carried away by yet more Denizens who wore huge, elbow-high padded gloves, a constantly moving line of them taking the gold to another corner, which looked like a brick yard, except with gold ingots instead of bricks stacked up everywhere. As soon as a Denizen unloaded his ingots he went back again in yet another line. Both moving lines of Denizens reminded Arthur very much of ants at work.

In addition to the heat and light, there was also a dull, mechanical thumping noise that pervaded the room. That came from one end, where an axle powered by the water-wheel outside turned a slightly smaller interior wheel that in turn drove a series of lesser wheels, belts, and pistons that powered an array of mechanical hammers. The largest hammer had a head about the size of a family car, and the smallest had a head about as big as Arthur's.

All the hammers were pounding away with monotonous regularity, Denizens busy around them, placing and snatching out gold that started as an ingot beneath the big hammer and ended up as a broad flat sheet by the time the smallest mechanical hammer was finished with it. From there the sheets of gold were taken by another line of Denizens to the farthest corner of the room, where two or three hundred workbenches were set up, each with a Denizen hammering away, making the sheets of gold even thinner.

There was constant activity everywhere, save for one area quite close to Arthur, where around fifty Denizens lay as if asleep, each with a narrow strip of pale blue parchment or paper stuck on their foreheads, extending down their noses to their necks.

Arthur looked quickly around at the workers and the odd sight of the papered Denizens, but didn't waste any time in asking what they were doing. He had more important things to worry about.

"Who's in charge here?" he asked. He had to shout to be heard over all the noise of the hammering, the Denizens calling out to one another and the gurgle and hiss of molten gold running along the gutter. "And is there any way to look outside to see what's happening?"

"You're really, truly not going to kill everyone?" asked Marek.

"No!" shouted Arthur. "Why do you keep asking? Do I look like some kind of crazy murderer?"

"No. . . ." Marek sounded as if he did still think that but didn't want to upset Arthur. "Forgive me. These are strange times . . . and I saw what you did to those Nithlings."

"Speaking of Nithlings, a whole lot more will be attacking here soon," Arthur warned. "I need to talk to whoever is in charge."

Marek said something, but Arthur couldn't hear it. Frustrated, he retreated back to the antechamber, gesturing to Marek to follow him. With the door half-closed, in the relative quiet, Arthur repeated his question yet again.

"I don't know who's in charge," said Marek, cringing

so low that his head was almost level with Arthur's. "None of the telephones work. We had a letter this morning saying Lady Friday has gone away and Friday's Dawn, our Guildmaster, went up the canal to find out what's happening. After he left we got a letter from Superior Saturday saying she has taken over the Middle House and we are all to keep at work, that a new Guildmaster will soon come to oversee us."

"Who's next in precedence within the House after Friday's Dawn?" asked Arthur. He was getting anxious about an imminent attack by Fetchers. "And is there any way to get a view from the tower of what's happening outside?"

"Elibazeth Flat Gold is the Master Foiler," said Marek. "But she is far too busy with the foil to interrupt. I am third, after Elibazeth, and responsible for collecting letters. Kemen is second, but he is experiencing and won't be back for weeks. To look out from the tower, it is a matter of opening this inner door differently. However, if you are not going to kill us or destroy anything, why don't you just leave? We have work to do!"

Arthur blinked. Marek had switched from cowardly groveling to strangely aggressive in the space of a breath.

"I'm Lord Arthur, Rightful Heir to the Architect, Commander of the Army of the Architect, and a whole lot of other stuff, and I'm taking command here, not Superior Saturday or anyone else. Understand?"

Marek immediately went back to cowardly groveling, sinking down on one knee as he answered, "Yes, Lord."

"Go and interrupt Elizabeth —"

"Elibazeth, lord."

"Elibazeth, then. Go and tell her I want any Denizens who have served in the Army to gather near the door here, with whatever weapons you have or can improvise. And open this door the 'different way' so I can take a look out of the tower."

"Yes, lord."

Marek showed Arthur how to pull out the door handle, rotate it ninety degrees, and push it back in. This time what lay beyond the open door was not the antechamber and the outer door, but a dim, cold, and very damp stairway, none of these conditions much relieved by the thin bands of light that came in through the gaps in the slats of the shuttered windows above.

Arthur bounded up the stairs as Marek shut the door behind him. Reaching the first window, the boy unbolted the shutters and opened one a few inches, enough to look out without being too obvious.

Through the narrow gap he saw the snowy plain and not much else. Visibility was still very limited, with snow falling steadily and the clouds almost low enough to touch from the tower. Arthur had half-expected to see massed ranks of Fetchers or other Nithlings, so he was relieved by the absence of enemies, even if it was only for the time being.

Then it occurred to him that he was looking out only one side of the tower. The Fetchers could be forming up on one of the other two sides, the fourth side being the canal, and thus probably safe. Unless the Fetchers had wings, or boats. Which was entirely possible, Arthur thought. So he would have to check that side as well.

To look out other windows he had to go up and look out at the next three levels. Each landing had a single window, to either north, east, south, or west — not that Arthur knew which one was which.

Arthur ran up the stairs and quickly looked out in each direction, making sure he refastened the shutters. He knew that back in the Secondary Realms the Fetchers — winged or otherwise — couldn't cross a threshold without invitation but he wasn't sure if that applied in the House.

Thinking of that reminded him of two things. One was that he hadn't actually confirmed his location. He assumed he was somewhere in the Middle House. The second was that even though he didn't want to consult it, Dame Primus still had his *Compleat Atlas of the House* and he felt a bit funny about that. He'd rather have it with him, so if he absolutely needed to he would be able to check things out in it. He also didn't want Dame Primus to have it.

It's not that I don't trust her, he thought. *It's just that . . . I'm not sure if I should trust her.*

Arthur shook his head and sighed. Thinking about the Will and its manifestation as the annoying Dame Primus wasn't helping the current situation.

Focus, he told himself. *Focus!*

There was nothing immediately threatening in any direction, or at least nothing that Arthur could see. He went back down somewhat slower than he'd gone up, but his mind was still running fast, thinking through the situation and what he was going to do. At the bottom, he returned to the antechamber, turned the handle around, and opened the door back on to the chamber of molten gold and all its workers.

Arthur had hoped that he'd immediately see a sizable force of former veterans of the Army parading ready to receive his orders, but that was not the case. Only three Denizens stood in line, at ease. They were carrying the ten-foot-long gold-scooping poles, with no other, more effective weapons in evidence. Everything else was much as it had been ten minutes before, a hive of activity, except that the group of Denizens lying down with paper or parchment strips stuck on their foreheads had gotten noticeably larger. At least another twenty or thirty Denizens had lain down in that area.

Marek was nowhere in sight, but a female Denizen who was wearing a ruffled green shirt, as well as a rather cleaner and more impressive apron than the others, was standing by the door, giving instructions to several workers. She turned as Arthur marched in, and bowed low.

"Elibazeth?" asked Arthur.

"Yes, lord."

"Is this *all* the Denizens here who have done Army service?"

"All who are not experiencing," said Elibazeth. She gestured to the sleeping, paper-stuck Denizens.

"What?" Arthur didn't think he'd heard her properly, over the noise of the hammers and everything.

"Experiencing."

"Experiencing what? Being asleep?"

"No, lord," said Elibazeth. "They are not asleep. They are partaking of mortal experience. They will wake in a month or two."

"What!" exclaimed Arthur. "What are those papers they've got stuck on?"

"Mortal experiences," said Elibazeth stolidly. She did not appear to be so overawed by Arthur as Marek had been. She was simply matter-of-fact. "They are pieces of mortal experience that Lady Friday has discarded. As they are not explicitly forbidden, they are allowed."

Arthur stared at her, then shook his head. Obviously he was going to have to get a lot more information, and as quickly as possible.

"Wait here," he instructed Elibazeth before he strode over to the pitifully small line of former soldiers.

"Ten-hut!" called the Denizen on the right. The trio came to attention.

"Present ar — !"

"Thanks!" called out Arthur. "We won't bother with all that. Stand easy! I'm Arthur, Commander of the Glorious Army of the Architect. Um, are there really only three of you here who've done military service?"

"Yes, sir!" answered the Denizen who'd been about to give the order to present arms. "That is, the only ones not experiencing, sir. There's probably twenty among the 'speriencers. Sir."

"Right. . . ." said Arthur. "We haven't got much time. What are your names, with former rank and unit, please?"

"Lance-Bombardier Jugguth Flat Gold of the Moderately Honorable Artillery Company," replied the right-hand Denizen. "I've only been out fifty years. This 'ere is Private

Lukin Flat Gold of the Regiment and Trooper Serelle Flat Gold of the Horde."

"Okay, Bombardier Jugguth. There is a force of Nithlings — Fetchers and maybe worse — nearby, who will probably attack soon. I want you to take your . . . ah . . . section into the tower and keep a lookout in all four directions. If you see anything, send someone to report to me at once. I'll be here with Elibazeth. Got that?"

"Yes, sir," shouted Jugguth. "Only as there's only three of us, how can we look in all four directions, sir?"

"Swap sides," said Arthur, biting back a sharper retort. "Check the canal side every five minutes for a minute or two, then go back to whichever side you're covering. Understand?"

"Yes, sir," said Jugguth, but Arthur wasn't absolutely sure the Denizen had understood. While the Bombardier marched his section out the door, Arthur ran over to Elibazeth, who was inspecting a large sheet of gold foil that had been brought to her by another Denizen. She had moved closer to the pool of molten gold, and it was much hotter there, hot enough to make sweat start to run down the back of Arthur's neck.

"Elibazeth!" Arthur interrupted a technical discussion about how much more hammering the foil needed. "How do you normally protect yourselves against Nithlings? I mean, the Lower House has Commissionaires and so on. What guards do you have here?"

"When Friday's Dawn is here, he is accompanied by a flight of Gilded Youths," said Elibazeth. She didn't sound very concerned about the prospect of being attacked. "They patrol the Flat and the First Ascent of the Canal, and dispose of any Nithling incursions. After sunfall, I believe the Winged Servants of the Night do likewise. However, the Gilded Youths have departed with our Guildmaster — that is to say, Friday's Dawn. I do not know if the Winged Servants will come with the night, or even if there will be a night. Day and night have been rather uncertain here since the weather has been broken. However, the mill itself is very securely built, the gate is much stronger than perhaps it appears, and we have other defenses. It would be *very* difficult for any Nithlings to get in."

Arthur wiped the sweat off his forehead and tried to gather his thoughts. It was good to hear that the defenses were strong. And he had sentries now, so at least he wasn't going to be surprised by a Nithling attack. What he needed to know now was . . . pretty much everything.

"Right. Let's start with the basics. Where exactly are we?"

Chapter Six

"An ambulatory seedpod," Milka told Leaf, gesturing to the smoking husk of the creature that had just been destroyed. "They get in from outside occasionally. If you're unlucky enough to see one again . . ."

"What do I do?" asked Leaf.

"Count yourself lucky that you mortals die easily," replied Milka grimly. "Denizens can live for months while the bloom grows in them."

Leaf didn't answer, but crossed to the other side of the corridor, to keep as far away as she could, even from the scorched fragments of the seedpod.

"Come on," ordered Milka to Leaf. "Leave that, Feorin! You don't have to wear it here."

Feorin stopped struggling with his trench coat and simply scrunched it under his arm. His wings turned in towards his spine and folded themselves flat, the tips withdrawing up from his knees to just below his waist.

Leaf wasn't sure how long it took to get to their destination. Every time Feorin hesitated or slowed, she felt an overpowering urge to jump back. The immediate fear of encountering another seedpod overlaid the more general anxiety of her situation; the shock of the sudden encounter had intensified her already nervous state. Leaf felt incredibly jumpy, even on the brink of breaking down. Only the knowledge that this would do no good at all helped her keep herself together.

"Feorin . . . stop," said Milka after a small, exasperated sigh. She pointed to a left-hand door Feorin had just passed. It had the number 18 above it, the numeral made of small blue stone chips. "This is it."

The room beyond the door was about as big as Leaf's living room back home. The far wall was dominated by a full-length window, the first Leaf had seen. It looked like frosted glass so Leaf couldn't see anything through it, though it did admit a great deal of purple-tinged sunlight that was bright enough to wash out the ubiquitous blue-flamed gas jets in the ceiling.

An old wooden table with one chair was in the center of the room; there was a bed in the corner, and a man — a normal mortal human from the look of him — was asleep on top of the covers, fully dressed in the same kind of green hospital uniform the cleaner back in the ward on Earth had worn.

"Is that her?" asked Feorin.

"Him," said Milka. "I told you they change them all the time. Wake up!"

The man sat up with a startled cry. He was quite old, Leaf saw. Older than her grandfather, his short hair white as paper.

"What?" he said. "I only just lay down!"

"We've brought you a sleeping waker," said Feorin.

"A waking sleeper," corrected Milka. "We need a receipt."

The man rubbed his eyes and looked at Leaf.

"Hi," he said. "I'm Harrison. I expect they've stuffed up again. You're a Piper's child, aren't you?"

"No . . ." said Leaf. She tried to act puzzled and disoriented, which wasn't hard. "I was in the hospital. . . ."

Harrison got out of the bed with a frown.

"But She never takes anyone under fifty!"

"We need a receipt!" interrupted Milka. "And quickly. We've got better things to do."

"Like drink tea," said Feorin.

"All right, all right!" Harrison shook his head several times, blinked, and wiped his eyes, then went over to the desk and quickly wrote something on a piece of paper, using a ballpoint pen. Milka took it and pursed her lips in distaste.

"Poor penmanship," she said. "Those pointy things are not proper writing instruments!"

"Will it do as a receipt?" asked Harrison.

"I suppose so," said Milka. She folded the paper very precisely into a square one-eighth of its original size and put it in her pocket. "Feorin! Come on."

The two Denizens stalked out, leaving Leaf standing in front of the desk. Harrison rubbed his eyes again and leaned forward, propping his chin on his hands for a moment, with his eyes closed as if he were asleep. Then he shook himself awake again, pushed the chair back, and stood up.

"I'm sorry," he said. "You'd better sit down. This is going to be a shock."

Leaf took the chair.

Harrison paced in front of the desk, scratching his head. Finally he stopped and turned to face Leaf.

"Look, I don't know how to tell you this. Uh, let's see . . . how can I put it? The two . . . ah . . . people who brought you here. Well, they're not human. They're like kind of aliens, called Denizens, and normally they live in a place . . . a world I guess . . . called the House. Only this isn't there, it's another planet somewhere in maybe the Lesser Magellanic Cloud, I think, or maybe . . . oh . . . I'm too tired to even think, let alone explain. Anyway, most of the real people here are asleep and they'll stay asleep until . . . but there are a few normal humans like me who are awake . . . but we're prisoners too. . . . Ah, I bet none of this is making sense. . . ."

"You say you're a prisoner here?" asked Leaf. She wanted to be sure he wasn't a willing servant of Lady Friday.

"Yeah," said Harrison. "I was dumb enough to take a job in 'Dr. Friday's' hospital back on Earth. Next thing I know . . . here I am, and here I've stayed. What year is it back home?"

Leaf told him. Harrison asked her again and she repeated it. He stood completely still the second time, the muscles working in his throat as if he were holding back a sob.

"Then I've been here for fourteen years. . . . I thought it was longer. Weird stuff happens when you go through the House between Earth and here."

"We got here via this House place?" asked Leaf.

"According to Axilrad," said Harrison. "One of the Denizens. She talks to me sometimes. Ah, what does it matter. . . . I'm stuck here, you're stuck here, we're better off than the sleepers. . . ."

"What happens to the sleepers?" Leaf felt her whole body tense up with that question, because she really meant "What's going to happen to my aunt?"

"You don't want to know," muttered Harrison. He kept pacing. "Really, you don't. You're bound to be in shock already; I don't want to make it worse."

"I *do* want to know," said Leaf. She took a deep breath, preparing herself for whatever she might be about to hear. "And I already know about the House and the Denizens and Lady Friday being a Trustee of the Will and all."

Harrison stopped pacing and stared at her.

"How? I mean, you are a human?"

"Yes," said Leaf. "But I've been in the House before. I'm a friend of Arthur, the Rightful Heir to the Architect."

"You mean Arthur's real?" Harrison sat down on the edge of the desk and looked directly at Leaf for the first time, his eyes suddenly lively, the weariness gone. "The Denizens talk about him sometimes. Axilrad said he doesn't exist, that there are always rumors about a Rightful Heir . . . but if he can defeat Lady Friday . . . maybe . . . there is a chance I can get home after all. . . ."

"He's real enough," said Leaf. "He's already beaten Mister Monday, Grim Tuesday, and Drowned Wednesday . . . and probably Sir Thursday too, only I don't know for sure. Now, tell me . . . what happens to the sleepers?"

Harrison looked away again and clicked his fingernails in agitation.

"She only used to bring across a dozen or so a month,"

he said. "I don't know why there's been this sudden influx. Thousands of them, and I have to turn them in their beds every twelve hours, until they . . . until it's time . . ."

His voice trailed off.

"Until it's time for what?" demanded Leaf.

"They go to Lady Friday," said Harrison. "Then —"

Whatever he was going to say next was interrupted by a sudden electronic squawk, followed by a crackle from the wooden box on Harrison's desk that Leaf had taken for a large paperweight or something, but was in fact an intercom.

"Harrison! I hear you've got new help. Get over to the Yellow Preparation Room now and set up a dozen for the boss."

"Axilrad," Harrison explained to Leaf. "The Denizen I work for. She's not so bad, compared to most of the others. Come on!"

"But what happens to the sleepers?" Leaf asked as Harrison hustled her to the door.

"You'll see," said Harrison. Despite his comment about Axilrad being not too bad, he seemed extremely fearful of keeping her waiting. "Follow me."

Harrison walked so fast he almost broke into a jog. Leaf kept up with him as best she could, though her legs were still not fully working and it took her much more effort than usual just to maintain a fast walk.

A hundred yards or so along the corridor, they passed a large rectangular window of clear glass set into the inner wall. Through it, Leaf could see a large circular lake a few hundred feet below, and for the first time she got a clear sense that all the corridors and rooms she'd been in were definitely in the crater wall of something like an extinct volcano.

Looking out the window and up, Leaf at first only saw the strange, purple sky. Then she noticed a delicate tracery of pale gold, in a crazed pattern arching up from the far rim of the crater. It appeared to be an ultra-thin wire or metal framework, but it took Leaf several more seconds to work out that there was glass or something like glass between the metal wires, and that together they made up a domed cap that sat over the whole crater — a dome that was at least a mile in diameter and three or four hundred yards high.

"Hurry up!" called Harrison. He'd gotten a long way in front while Leaf was gawking out the window. The girl stopped sightseeing and ran after him. But when she'd caught up, she slowed again. The lake in the middle of the crater had reminded her of something. It was a large body of water, easily big enough to sail a small craft on.

Water . . . lake . . . sea . . . boat . . . ship . . . Mariner, thought Leaf.

She let Harrison get ahead again. She didn't stop; she just slowed her pace so that he disappeared around the curve in front of her. Then she pulled out the Mariner's medallion on its rather sad twined necklace of dental floss and raised it near her mouth.

"Please help me," she whispered to the small whale-bone disc. "It's Leaf here, Arthur's friend. He gave me the medallion. Please help me. I'm a prisoner of Lady Friday's, somewhere in the Secondary Realms. Please help. Or tell Arthur. Or Suzy Turquoise Blue. Please help."

She managed to repeat this almost-mantra several times before Harrison came into sight again, waiting outside a door marked 5. He frowned at Leaf, waited till she was only a few feet away, then knocked. He didn't wait for a reply, but opened it straight away and went in. Leaf followed more cautiously, worried about what she was going to see.

The Yellow Preparation Room was indeed yellow, having daisy-colored walls and a brighter, egg-yolk-colored ceiling. A large, rectangular chamber about the same size as Leaf's school gymnasium, it contained thirty of the same basic beds as had occupied Friday's hospital back on Earth, and all the beds were occupied by sleepers. Leaf quickly looked at the closest, to see if she recognized anyone, particularly Aunt Mango. But no one looked familiar. They were all quite old.

A Denizen stood in the middle of the room, behind a wooden table that was loaded with numerous bottles of different sizes and shapes, each containing a mysterious-looking fluid. A female Denizen, wearing an old-fashioned Florence Nightingale getup, complete with a starched white hat that made her even taller. While she was very attractive and at least six feet tall without the hat, she was not awe-inspiringly beautiful, or much taller than normal, so Leaf figured her to be only a mid-ranking servant of Lady Friday. She was intent on pouring a rich blue fluid from a bottle with a very long neck into a measuring cup, and didn't immediately look up as Harrison and Leaf came in.

"Um, excuse me, Axilrad, we're here," said Harrison, ducking his head in a little nervous bow.

Axilrad tipped the measuring cup into another bottle, then looked up and saw Leaf. Her frown of concentration immediately deepened. She put the bottle and measuring cup on the table and strode over to the girl.

"You're no sleeper! You're much too young! What are you?"

"I'm Leaf. I was asleep and I woke up —"

Axilrad reached out and gripped Leaf's chin, turning her face up to the gas flare in the ceiling.

"You're a Piper's child, aren't you? Who sent you? What is your purpose?"

"I was in the hospital and Dr. Friday came and then I must have gone to sleep again —"

Axilrad let go, and Leaf felt her neck twinge as her head dropped back to its normal position.

"This is odd," said the Denizen. She didn't look at Leaf, but spoke as if to herself. "She never takes anyone so young. There must be a reason. I shall have to go find out. I do not like a surprise of this sort."

"What's a Piper's —" Leaf started to ask, though the question didn't sound all that convincing, even to herself. Axilrad ignored her, instead striding to the door, barking out a command as she left.

"Harrison, prepare a dozen sleepers. The cordial is made up, in the checkered bottle. They are to go to the crater as soon as they're ready. I will be back soon, but do not wait for me. Get the girl to assist you. She is not to go out of your sight."

"Yes, ma'am," said Harrison. He bowed to the closed door. Leaf watched him with a sinking feeling. The man behaved like a slave and he wasn't likely to be much help for anything.

"Look at each sleeper," instructed Harrison. "They need to be lying on their backs. If they're not faceup, turn them so they are."

"Why?" asked Leaf. She walked over to the door and tried the handle, but it was locked.

"Just do it!" squeaked Harrison. He hurried to the table and picked up a silver spoon with a very long handle and a bottle with a checkered pattern in the glass. It was full of a sludgy fluid the color of dead grass.

"I'm not doing anything unless you tell me why," said Leaf. There was one other door, down the far end. She started to walk towards it.

"She'll punish both of us if they're not ready," said Harrison. He moved to the closest sleeper — a woman — and poured a measure of the brown-green fluid into the spoon, which he then expertly slipped into the woman's mouth. She swallowed and then immediately shivered and sat up, without opening her eyes.

Harrison quickly poured the mixture into two more sleepers, then had to set the bottle and spoon down to turn over the third, who was sleeping on his side. As he poured another spoonful, he spoke.

"The mixture raises them from a very deep, coma-like sleep to a higher level, where they can be given commands and move. When they're ready, I will order them to walk out that door, which leads to the crater."

"This door?" asked Leaf, who had been about to open it.

"Yes," said Harrison. "You can't escape, you know. There's nowhere to go. Even if you could leave the mountain, the plants would get you. You have no idea how horrible —"

"Yes I do," said Leaf. "How often do those seedpods get in?"

"Give me a hand and I'll try to answer your questions," grunted Harrison. He was turning another sleeper, a very large and heavy man.

Leaf looked at him, then at the sleepers, and shook her head.

"I'm not helping you help Lady Friday kill these people," she said. "Or whatever it is she does."

"That's what you say now," said Harrison. "I tried that too, when I first came here. But if you want to eat and drink and have somewhere safe to sleep, you'll soon change your tune."

Leaf didn't answer. She'd forgotten they weren't in the House and so would actually need sustenance. In fact, just the mention of eating and drinking made her feel suddenly thirsty. But it wasn't enough to get her to help out Harrison. She'd have to be a lot thirstier to help someone prepare a whole bunch of innocent people to get killed . . . or worse.

Instead she tried to think of a plan. She couldn't count on the Mariner's help. If he came at all it would probably be too late.

I have to find Aunt Mango, she thought. *Then I have to hide us both away and get in contact with Arthur or Suzy. But what can I do for everyone else? I have to try to do something. Maybe I should try to find a telephone to the House first. . . .*

"Right, they're ready," said Harrison. He went back to the table and picked up a small silver cone, which Leaf had assumed was a funnel. But he used it as a loudhailer, bringing it up to his mouth to speak in the narrow end.

"Sit up!" he called, and the silver cone changed his voice so that he sounded like Lady Friday when she had called the sleepers from their beds before, though this call was weaker and softer. Once again Leaf felt the words reverberate inside her head, but the compulsion was easy to ignore this time.

To the sleepers it was a command and, as one, they all immediately sat up.

"Slide off the bed and stand up!"

Leaf could only imagine what came next.

Chapter Seven

"We are in the Foil Mill of the Guild of Gilding and Illumination, on the Flat of the Middle House," said Elibazeth in a distracted tone, as if she were answering a child's question while concentrating on something else.

"Right," said Arthur. He gestured for her to continue, but Elibazeth offered no more information, instead looking with a critical eye at the Denizens scooping gold.

"I need to know more than that," Arthur continued, shouting louder. The constant beat of the hammers was really getting to him. "What's the 'Flat of the Middle House' and is there a map I can look at? I need to get to Lady Friday's Scriptorium, wherever that is — and I need to get there fast."

"I am very busy, Lord Arthur," replied Elibazeth. She turned to look down at him. "The gilders at Letterer's Lark and at the Aspect use more than four thousand hands of foil a day and I am the responsible guild officer —"

"The quicker you answer my questions, the quicker you can go back to your normal work," said Arthur coldly.

"If the Nithlings let you. Now, do you have a map of the Middle House?"

"Oh, very well," said Elibazeth. "Come into my office."

She walked towards the stacks of golden ingots. Arthur followed her, swallowing an angry complaint. No matter how many times he had to deal with Denizens, their single-mindedness about their jobs and their general lack of common sense when faced with things out of their ordinary experience always irritated him.

Elibazeth led Arthur down a very narrow lane between walls of golden bricks that ended at a wooden-framed door with a frosted window that had had *M_ster Foil_r* written on it in flaking gold letters.

Though its walls were still gold ingots, the office behind the door had a wood-paneled ceiling, was large and comfortable, and, most important to Arthur, it was much quieter. The sound of the hammers was only a distant vibration that he could feel more than hear.

Elibazeth went and sat behind the red leather-topped mahogany desk and began to rummage in the drawers. Arthur stood, ignoring both the simple wooden chair that faced the desk and the worn leather chaise lounge with the diamond-pattern rug over it.

"Here we are," said Elibazeth. She used her forearm to push the various documents on the desk to one side, then unfolded a small map in the cleared area.

Arthur bent over it and frowned. All he could see were disconnected, meaningless squiggles. Elibazeth frowned too, and rapped the paper with her knuckles. The squiggles quickly organized themselves to show a three-dimensional drawing of the side of a mountain whose steep slopes were interrupted by three wide plateaus.

"This is the Middle House," continued the Denizen, waving her hand over the whole mountainside. She pointed to the lowest and widest plateau, and the map obediently zoomed in, changed the perspective to an aerial view, and revealed several named locations, marked by dots of gold. "This is the Flat, where we are now. It falls under the jurisdiction of the Guild of Gilding and Illumination and its principle places of work are the Foil Mill here, the Hall of Excellent Aspect here, Letterer's Lark, and Ribboner's Redoubt here. Our place of repose is the town of Aurianburg, which you can see lies equidistant from the workshops."

"What's this line that goes up the mountainside from here to the next flat bit and the top one?" Arthur asked. He pointed and the map switched views again, back to the three-dimensional cross-section. "A road?"

"It is the Extremely Grand Canal," said Elibazeth. "It is used to move records between the three guilds and the storage lake, prior to their completion and removal to the Lower House to be archived."

"But it goes up the mountainside," said Arthur. "Does the water flow uphill?"

"The canal moves textually charged water," said Elibazeth, with a bored sigh. "It is divided into regular currents that move up and down at various speeds. Anything with writing or type on it will be taken by the current. We do not have a lot to do with the canal here. Our foil is taken overland by hand to Letterer's Lark, and smaller quantities —"

"Right, right," interrupted Arthur. He didn't want to know about where the foil went. "What is the next flat level called? And where is Lady Friday's Scriptorium?"

"The next plateau is called the Middle of the Middle," sniffed Elibazeth. "It is the domain of the Guild of Illustration and Augmentation, and a nastier bunch you'll never meet, unless you go up to the Top Shelf, where the so-called High Guild of Binding and Restoration laze about. I understand that Lady Friday's Scriptorium is actually beyond that, on the mountain peak, but as to the truth of that, I cannot say. Now can I get back to my work?"

"Is there any way to go directly to the Top Shelf?" asked Arthur.

"Normally you could take an elevator," said Elibazeth. "Though why you would, I don't know. But the elevators aren't working. I expect they're broken, like the weather. Now I must really insist —"

"Just a few more questions," said Arthur. "Is it possible for people . . . or Denizens . . . to travel on the canal? And have you ever heard anything about a Part of the Architect's Will being hidden in the Middle House?"

"Questions about the nature and workings of the canal are best put to the Paper Pushers who work the canal. I know nothing about the Architect's Will, other than that a particularly fine gold foil was made for it some eleven thousand years ago. We still have a sample here. I can show you, as the Rightful Heir, though we do not normally reveal it to outsiders. It is of note for several reasons —"

"No, that's okay," said Arthur hurriedly. But Elibazeth had already pressed a corner of the desk, revealing a small secret drawer. She slid in her hand and drew out a tiny crystal prism, no larger than her little finger, and handed it to the boy. Arthur took it with some puzzlement.

"Where's the foil?" he asked.

"Hold it to the light," said Elibazeth.

Arthur turned the prism so that it caught the light and

saw that there was a tiny speck of gold suspended in the very middle of the prism.

"She came and made it Herself," said Elibazeth reverently. "The Architect. She gave us that leftover piece."

"Did you see the actual Will?" asked Arthur curiously. "The document, I mean. Did the Architect gild the letters here?"

"No, She took the foil away," said Elibazeth. "Now, if I may have that back —"

Arthur slowly shook his head. He was interested in the foil now, because he had remembered something Dr. Scamandros had talked about once: how things that had once been together but then separated could be sorcerously linked, that one could affect the other. Perhaps this speck of foil could be used to track the parts of the Will that had been gilded by the Architect. Not that he knew how to do that, but if he could get in touch with Scamandros . . .

"I think I might be able to use it," he said.

"But it is the guild's most important treasure!" protested Elibazeth. "Surely —"

"I might need it!" snapped Arthur. It felt surprisingly good to snap at the Denizen, his display of anger lessening some of the tension that had built up inside him. Though it also felt a bit wrong. It was bad behavior, and his mother would definitely not approve. But he had to make the

Denizens cooperate, and surely his mother would understand; after all, she was in danger and he had to do whatever it took to rescue her.

Arthur tried to stop thinking about his mother.

I have to focus, he thought. *I can't waste time thinking about unnecessary things. I have a mission and I'll carry it out, just like I was taught at Fort Transformation. Forget about anything but the mission.*

"I'm also going to need some warmer clothes. Have you got any warm coats?"

"No," said Elibazeth. "We are warmed by our gold. If there is nothing else you wish to learn . . . or *take* . . . Lord Arthur, I must insist on returning to work."

"What about wings?" Arthur didn't want to try flying through snow and cloud, but the weather might improve. A good pair of wings might get him quickly up to the Scriptorium. "Have you got any?"

"We have no wings at all," said Elibazeth firmly.

She got up from behind the desk and walked out. Arthur followed her, his mind still occupied with trying to work out what to do. Since flying was apparently out, the canal seemed the best option for getting higher up the mountain, but he would freeze without better clothes. There was also the likelihood of attack by the Nithlings and other enemies. It would be best to keep moving, to avoid a direct confrontation.

"Hey, Elibazeth!" he called out as they entered the gold-pouring chamber and the noise and heat assailed him once more. "Where can I find some Paper Pushers? And have you got any spare leather aprons?"

Elibazeth turned back with a frown. "The Paper Pushers maintain a wharf a half parsang west of the mill," she said, pointing in a direction that Arthur quickly revised from what he had been calling south. "Aprons are for approved guild members only —"

"I need two," interrupted Arthur. He figured he could wear one in front and one behind, kind of like a cloak. The aprons were thick leather — they'd insulate him and keep the snow off. They might provide enough protection to save him from hypothermia without having to resort to the powers of the Key.

"I suppose in your case we must make an exception," said Elibazeth. She clapped her hands, a surprisingly sharp sound that cut through the bass rumble of the hammers. A Denizen returning from unloading ingots ran over, listened to her instruction, then ran off to fetch several thick leather aprons for Arthur.

"Now, I really must get on," said Elibazeth. She bowed

her head and stalked over to the pool of gold, going far closer to the molten metal than Arthur would be able to without sorcerous protection.

Arthur took his aprons and walked quickly back to the door. He was almost there when it opened and Jugguth rushed in. He saw Arthur, slid to a halt, and saluted.

"They're coming, sir! From the south!"

"How many? How far away?" Arthur slid the apron over his head and did up the ties, then put the other one on backwards and tied it at the front. Because they were made for Denizens, they came down almost to his ankles — it looked a bit like he was wearing a leather dress, but Arthur didn't care.

"Three, sir!"

"Three!? Only three Fetchers?"

"No, no, not Fetchers, sir. I don't know what they are. Two are your size, and one is about twice as big and much wider. They have on uniforms, sir."

"What color uniforms?" Arthur asked quickly.

"Pale yellow coats, a fair bit of white in the pigment," said Jugguth. "With big black fuzzy hats. One has a long spear."

"New Nithling uniforms," said Arthur. "One of the Piper's near-Denizens with two Piper's children . . . I wonder . . . Anyway, how far away are they?"

"They'll be outside by now," said Jugguth. "I watched them for a long time to make sure I knew what I was looking at. You can take a look through the mail slot if you like."

Arthur sighed.

So much for a quick getaway before any enemies arrive, he thought.

"I'll take a look," he said. "You go back up and watch out for anyone else, and this time, come and tell me as soon as you see something."

"Yes, sir!" shouted Jugguth. He saluted and spun around so fast that he lost his balance and almost cannoned into Arthur, who had to step back. The Denizen spun around twice more before stopping himself and running back through the doorway. Arthur waited for him to go through and shut the door, then moved the handle to gain entry to the portico and went through himself.

Someone was knocking on the outer door. A polite *rat-a-tat-tat,* not the smashing blows of a weapon.

"Hello, anyone home?" asked someone outside. The voice echoed through the mail slot.

Arthur frowned and cocked his head to one side. The speaker sounded familiar, though he couldn't quite place it, with the echo. He walked forward, careful to stay out of line with the mail slot, which he noted was open. He didn't want to be stuck by a spear through that gap.

But he could be seen, and there was a sharp intake of breath on the other side of the door.

"Arthur?" asked the voice. "Arthur!?"

"Suzy!"

Arthur took a step, ready to open the door, then stopped himself. It sounded like Suzy, but he couldn't be sure. Even if it was her, she might have been sorcerously forced to obey the Piper and would treat Arthur as an enemy. Jugguth had described New Nithling uniforms and one of the three outside must be one of the Piper's soldiers.

There was a muffled exchange beyond the door, then another voice sounded through the mail slot.

"Ray . . . I mean, Arthur . . . it's me, Fred. Can you let us in? It's freezing out here."

Fred and Suzy, thought Arthur. *With a New Nithling soldier.*

"Stand back!" Arthur called out. He waited till he heard footsteps crunching in the snow, then he gingerly crouched down a foot or so away from the mail slot and looked out . . . hoping for the best and expecting the worst.

Chapter Eight

It was getting dark outside. The sun — or *suns,* since there might be more than one high above the clouds — was setting. In the twilight, made still darker by the steady fall of snow, Arthur studied the faces of the two Piper's children and the male Denizen or New Nithling who stood between them.

The two children certainly looked like Suzy Turquoise Blue and Fred Initial Numbers Gold, but they were in the uniforms of the Piper's army, and the soldier between them was definitely a New Nithling. He appeared to be a Denizen at first, but Arthur saw that he had seven fingers on each hand and the small dent in the middle of his forehead under the black fur hat was not a bruise but a third eye, a quarter the size of the other two.

Arthur looked out for ten long seconds, blinking his eyes against the cold wind that blew in through the slot. He didn't know what to do, or think. He badly wanted to let Suzy and Fred in, but he couldn't help remembering what Dame Primus had said: All the Piper's children were suspect . . . and he was alone.

Finally, he looked away. Staring at the ground, he spoke.

"I don't think I can let you in. You're in the Piper's uniform, so you serve him now."

"Not on purpose!" called out Suzy. "He made us wear the uniforms, but he never got around to ordering us to do anything else. It's me, Suzy Turquoise Blue! I never do what I'm told anyway. I'm definitely not going to obey the Piper . . . ah . . . urg . . ."

Arthur looked out again. Suzy was on her knees in the snow, struggling with a rope or something that was around her neck. Arthur couldn't quite see it, but it was strangling her. Fred was trying to get his fingers under it without success, but the Nithling soldier was paying no attention, instead looking back out across the snowy plain.

"Of course she'll obey!" shouted Fred. "We both will! We'll follow orders! Nod your head, Suzy!"

Suzy nodded desperately. Fred let go of the noose or stranglecord, and the girl took a huge intake of breath and then burst into a paroxysm of coughing.

"What was that?" asked Arthur.

Fred pulled his collar down and took a few paces closer to the door. Arthur still couldn't see clearly, but there was something around Fred's neck. A thin line of writing — a tattoo perhaps.

"The Piper put a spell on us," said Fred. "If we disobey a direct order, or talk about disobeying, it chokes us. But we were never ordered to attack you, Arthur, or anything like that. We got away first. Can we come in and get warm and talk?"

Arthur hesitated. He really wanted to have Fred and Suzy as friends again, and talk over everything. But he just couldn't be sure they could be trusted.

"What about the New Nithling soldier?" he asked.

"Banneret Ugham?" croaked Suzy as she staggered to her feet and massaged her throat. "He says he's only been ordered to look after us and so that's what he's going to do. You haven't been ordered to attack Arthur or anything, have you, Uggie?"

"I have no present quarrel with Lord Arthur," said Ugham. His voice was surprisingly high and rather flute-like, quite at odds with his size and fearsome appearance. In addition to his charged spear, he had a broad-bladed sword hanging from the left side of his belt and a knife with a bronze knuckle-duster hilt on the right. A big knuckle-duster, to cater for his seven fingers.

Arthur noted that Suzy and Fred also had knuckle-duster knives on their belts, smaller ones, scaled to fit their hands. So if they were enemies, he'd be facing three blades at the least.

"Indeed, it may be such that we face a common foe and should join hands with Lord Arthur against this enemy," Ugham continued, pointing with his spear at a vast line of hundreds of Fetchers that had suddenly come into sight about a hundred yards away, a dark mass of Nithlings stark against the snow. They marched forward a few paces and then stopped and somewhere behind them came a distant, disturbing shout from something that sounded neither human, Denizen, nor Fetcher — a kind of squealing shriek that was suddenly stifled, as if a muzzle had been applied. The sound of it made the Fetchers quiver in their ranks and sent a visible shiver through Fred and Suzy. Arthur felt it himself. There was just something *wrong* about it.

"I'm in favor," croaked Suzy.

"Aye!" called out Fred.

Both of them came closer to the door and together said, "Arthur?"

I really hope this isn't a trick, thought Arthur. *I guess if I absolutely have to, I can use the Key. . . .*

"Aye," he said, and he lifted the beam and slid back the locking bolts.

All three were inside a minute later. Suzy clapped Arthur on the back, but Fred just nodded firmly, looking him in the eye, their gaze that of two soldiers who have met again in trying circumstances. Ugham bowed to Arthur, then immediately helped to re-bar and bolt the door, before crouching to keep watch through the mail slot.

"Thanks, Arthur. It's good to get out of that snow," said Suzy with a shiver. "Beats me why Fred's lot like it so much here."

"We don't like the snow," said Fred. "The weather's been busted for years. Not to mention the diurnal cycle."

"What's that?" asked Suzy.

"The routine of day and night," said Fred. "We had a year of night once, before someone got the sun up again."

"It's good to see you," said Arthur gruffly. "I thought . . . I thought I might not, after you were captured."

"Oh, well, we're just like bad pennies," said Suzy cheerfully. "Always turn up when least expected. Like those Fetchers outside. Whose are they, do you know? Can we go properly inside? Somewhere with a fire?"

She started to turn the handle of the inner door, but Arthur intervened.

"No, it's too noisy in there. Let's talk for a minute here, if the Fetchers aren't advancing."

"Methinks they wait for some commander or personage of note," said Ugham. "I have not bickered with

Fetchers afore now. I have heard word of them as minor servants, sent forth to seek and steal. They would be unworthy opponents for such as we, save they come in such numbers as valor could not withstand."

"I wonder what they're waiting for," said Fred. "What was that horrible scream?"

"They're probably waiting for Saturday's Dusk or one of her other main servants," Arthur ventured. "Though the Dusk I met in the Pit didn't sound like that. We'd better not waste time. . . . What I want to know is how you got here. Why did the Piper send you two here . . . and, er, Banneret Ugham, of course? What happened after you were captured?"

"Uh, the Piper didn't send us," said Fred, his forehead knotted into a frown. "It's a bit of a long story. I suppose I'd better start at the beginning, though I'm a bit hazy about the start — everything went black for me when the Piper came up the ramp —"

"Me too," interrupted Suzy. "I just conked out when I heard his pipe. Dunno what happened then."

"You all went completely still," said Arthur. "Like statues. Sir Thursday went into the Improbable Stair and I went with him, but I threw the pocket in the Spike first, which was just as well, because it blew the Spike up or something so the Maze could move again."

"We knew the Spike had gone, later on, because the New Nithlings told us," said Fred. "That was when I woke up again, in their camp, with this thing on my throat."

He pointed to the line around his neck. On closer examination, Arthur could see that it was a tattoo, or perhaps writing in some kind of indelible ink. Bending closer still, he could just make out the tiny letters and the words they made up. Like the letters in the Will, these ones also moved and shimmered and changed alphabets and were therefore even more difficult to read.

" 'I will serve . . . and obey . . . the Piper to my . . . last breath,' " Arthur read.

"One of the Newniths . . . what they call themselves . . . told me that's what it said," continued Fred. "They treated me . . . all of us . . . pretty well, though they made us wear these uniforms and they kept us locked up. Ugham was our guard. That was because the Piper had left for somewhere else and hadn't given us any instructions. I guess after about twelve hours, or more maybe, he came back and we were taken in to see him. He was furious about something, but was kind of weird about it. He kept breaking things and throwing his arms up and down but he was whispering, not shouting. It was really hard to hear him. That went on for a while, then this Denizen got dragged in by the guards. He said he had a message from Lady Friday about abdicating and leaving the Key —"

"Yeah, I got that message too," Arthur chimed in.

"Then he tried to give the Piper this metal tablet, but the Piper made him drop it on the ground and told no one to touch it because it was probably a nefarious device. One of the Newniths opened up the package with a spear point and the Piper was talking about it when Suzy whispered to me —"

"I said, 'I reckon that's a Transfer Plate,' " said Suzy. "So I jumped for it and Fred jumped after me and Ugham tried to catch both of us and so we were all connected when I touched the plate . . . and here we are. Is there a fire inside? Or some hot water? I think my fingers might be about to drop off."

"Lady Friday's messenger," asked Arthur. "Did you hear him say that the Fifth Key has been left in Friday's Scriptorium, for me or Saturday or the Piper?"

"Yes," said Fred. Suzy nodded. Ugham turned back from the mail slot for a moment to also nod gravely.

"Part Five of the Will is somewhere here in the Middle House too," continued Arthur. "At least Friday's message said so. I suppose none of it may be true."

"I reckon the Piper believed it," said Suzy. "About the

Key anyway. Just before we jumped, he was whispering away with his generals about how to seize it first."

"I guess Superior Saturday believes it's here as well," added Arthur. "Those Fetchers must be hers. . . . She controls the elevators; she can send anything down here. Which reminds me — I wonder where my look-outs are."

He looked up at the ceiling in puzzlement, then shook his head.

"Uh, I forgot, they've probably gone to report in the main chamber. This door can lead into two places, depending on which way you turn the handle."

"Let's go to the warm place, then," said Suzy. "I wonder if they've got any tea."

"What are the Fetchers doing?" asked Arthur.

"They stand in some disorder," said Ugham. "But perchance I spy some other . . . yes . . . a Superior Denizen alights from the cloud. His wings are silver."

"Saturday's Dusk, probably," said Arthur. "That's not good."

"Old silver wings? The Lieutenant Keeper saw him off when I was in the Door," said Suzy. "So you should have no trouble, Arthur, with the Key."

"You know I don't want to use the Key," said Arthur

sharply. "We'd better get inside and ask if there's another way out."

He turned the handle and opened the door — but instead of opening onto the main gold pool chamber it opened onto the gloomy interior of the tower.

"I must have done it wrong," said Arthur. He shut the door, turned the handle the other way, and opened the door again, but once more there was only the tower interior beyond.

"Were you expecting something else?" asked Suzy.

"Yes," snapped Arthur. "The inner chamber! Elibazeth said they had other defenses. I guess this is one. I'll ask my sentries."

He started up the steps with Suzy and Fred following, but by the time they reached the first landing, he knew from the silence above that Jugguth and the other two Denizens had probably gone back inside the main chamber — and Elibazeth had then closed it off. Running up to the next two landings proved this to be the case. The tower was deserted and the only way out was back down and through the front door.

The only obvious way out, thought Arthur. *But perhaps there is another exit after all. . . .*

"What are the Fetchers doing?" he shouted downstairs,

at the same time as he opened one of the shutters on the north side of the tower.

"They still stand like the cattle they are," reported Ugham. "But the silver-wing'd Denizen comes forward, bearing aloft a white cloth. He seeks a parley, methinks. Doubtless he fears they have not the strength to carry the day against Lord Arthur's Key."

Arthur looked out the window, onto the groaning, ice-edged waterwheel, a huge and menacing machine made somehow scarier by the gathering darkness beyond. He watched it turn. If it was slow enough, he thought it would be possible to climb out onto one of the flat spokes and be carried and slide down to the ground, out of sight of the Fetchers on the southern and eastern side. Or he'd fall into the canal and drown or get frozen to death.

It was slow enough, Arthur reckoned, though it would still be a dangerous path to the canal bank. But then the only other way would be to fight through the Fetchers and Saturday's Dusk, and Arthur was not confident about doing that. At least not without using the full powers of the Key.

"Ugham!" shouted Arthur. "Tell Saturday's Dusk you have to go inside to get me. Tell him to come back in half an hour. That should give us a reasonable head start."

"What are we going to do?" asked Fred.

Arthur pointed out the window.

"We're going to climb out onto a spoke of the wheel and get carried down, jumping off just before it hits the water. Then we'll head west along the canal to where the Paper Pushers are."

"Hmmph," said Suzy. "Back into the cold, in other words."

"Yes," confirmed Arthur. "Back into the cold."

Chapter Nine

Leaf shivered as the sleepwalkers slid off their beds and formed a line in obedience to Harrison's orders. There was something awful and creepy about their unseeing, half-open eyes and their floppy movements. Almost as if they were like perfect string puppet representations of humans, only with invisible strings.

"Follow me!" called out Harrison, and he walked to the far door. Lowering the silver cone, he added in his own weak voice, "You too, Leaf! Bring up the rear."

"What if I don't?" Leaf asked rebelliously. She tried to project a more aggressive tone than she felt, but she sounded weak and childish, even to herself.

"I can make the sleepers bring you," said Harrison. "Though they would hurt themselves in the process. Please, it would be easier for everyone if you just come along."

"I'm not helping you take these people to get killed," said Leaf.

"They don't get killed," said Harrison, but he didn't look at Leaf when he spoke. "They'll still be alive at the end of the day. After She's finished with them. Come on! We'll both get punished if we're late."

"I'm not cooperating," said Leaf. "But I want to see what's outside, so I guess I'll come along."

"You'll learn," said Harrison sourly. He slid back the two bolts securing the outside door and then wrestled with the long handle, the sound of a large and stiff lock clicking back inside. Then he pushed the door open, using his shoulder and grunting with the effort, as the door was several inches thick and the outer face was lined with steel plate.

Purple light streamed in, casting an unattractive glow over the faces of Harrison and the sleepers. Leaf slitted her eyes, not because it was too bright, just that the color was too intense, and it made her feel slightly ill.

It was warmer out in the purple sunlight, and a light breeze ruffled Leaf's hair, bringing with it a strange, slightly earthy scent, reminiscent of forests she'd walked in previously but overlaid with something like an exotic spice.

There was smooth gray rock underfoot, whorled in patterns to show it had once been lava, long cooled. The rock shelved down gently to the lake in the middle, which looked like normal water, though it too was tinged purple by the light.

Leaf looked around and saw that the crater wall reached

up three or four hundred feet. It was dotted with windows of various sizes and there were some doors high up as well, with suspended walkways hugging the cliff between them. Farther around the crater, probably where the twelve would be on the notional clock-face scheme, there was a broad iron balcony just below where the dome began. A spiral stair of red wrought iron ran down from the balcony all the way to the crater floor.

"Hurry up!" called Harrison. He was leading the sleepers down to the lakeshore and they had gotten thirty or forty yards ahead while Leaf stared up at the crater walls and the dome.

Leaf ignored him and continued to look around. Apart from the door they had come out, there were at least a dozen crater-level doors spaced around the rim. But they would probably all lead back into Lady Friday's complex, and so offered nothing useful. Or worse, they might lead to the jungle beyond the mountain. After encountering the walking seedpod, Leaf totally believed Milka that she didn't want to go there.

She also didn't want to see what was going to happen to the sleepers, but there didn't appear to be any alternative. The crater was all featureless gray stone, without an outcrop or anything to hide behind. Unless she could breathe underwater, the lake was out.

"Come on!" Harrison was down at the lakeshore now, ordering the sleepers to stand in a line facing the water. Or, as Leaf now saw, facing a slim pillar of darker stone that rose up in the very center of the lake, and so was also in the very center of the crater. It was about twenty feet wide at the water and ended in a flat top about four feet wide some fifteen feet above the level of the lake.

Leaf started heading over to Harrison, but she still kept looking for somewhere to hide. As she walked, she noticed movement up on the balcony at the twelve o'clock position. Several Denizens were flexing their wings — wings that were not discolored by the purple sunlight. They were bright yellow, the color of daisy heads. Leaf watched four of them launch from the balcony. They carried a chair suspended on ropes beneath them, a silver chair with a high, curving back that looked almost like a throne.

A picnic throne, Leaf thought. *And no points for guessing who that's for. . . .*

She slowed again and looked once more for a hiding spot. Harrison was fussing around with the last of his sleepers, tilting an old woman's head back so that, like the others, she was looking at the spire in the lake.

Leaf saw a crack in the stone, a shadow that might be just wide enough for her to climb into. She ran over to it and knelt down. It was a very narrow crevasse, but she thought it was a little wider than she was at the top, and it was broader below. It was also only four feet deep, but it looked like there was a hole in one corner that might lead deeper.

She took a breath and climbed down. It was a tight squeeze and she grazed her hip as she twisted around, but then she was in. Leaf sighed and crawled to the hole. As she'd hoped, it led farther into the stony ground — it was impossible to say how far, as the purple sunlight only lit up the first part of the hole and it clearly went much deeper. Deep into darkness.

She was about to crawl in anyway when she smelled something familiar. Familiar yet repulsive, an odor that made her instantly flinch, even though she didn't immediately recognize it. It was a damp, rotten kind of smell and it made the gorge rise in her throat, and that was what made her remember when she'd smelled it before.

The mind-control mold she'd thrown up had smelled just like what she was smelling now. . . .

Leaf recoiled, this time scraping the skin off her elbows as she tried to squirm out of the narrow crack even faster than she'd gone in. As she hoisted herself up, a thin tendril of gray fungus came quivering out of the dark and slowly felt around the spot where her feet had been only a few seconds before.

Leaf threw herself back and landed badly, hurting herself. But she didn't stop, scuttling back with a sobbing cry to find herself at the feet of Harrison. He helped her up as she cried out.

"Fungus! The mind-control fungus!"

"The gray creeper?" said Harrison. "The spores do get in occasionally and root in the cracks. It's not so bad, that one. It'll only give you nightmares. Still, I'll report it. One of the guards will burn it out. Come on — we have to get back a safe distance."

Leaf followed him meekly. The smell of the gray fungus was still everywhere in her nose and mouth. She could taste it and she could remember the terrible pressure in her head when it was establishing itself —

She stopped to dry retch for a moment, but Harrison came back and pulled her along by her wrist.

"Come on! They've put the chair down. She'll fly down any minute and we have to be back almost to the door or we might get caught up too!"

The two of them scrambled back to the door and Leaf collapsed, coughing. Her legs ached and her mouth felt horrible, made no better by the loose threads that stuck to her tongue as she dragged the sleeve of her robe across her face. Leaf spat them out, in the process looking up and out across the lake.

The silver chair was on the pillar of dark stone. The four Denizens hovered in formation around it; the lake roiled underneath from the downbeat of their wings.

High on the balcony, a star flashed into being, or so it seemed to Leaf. A light too bright to look at, that leaped into the air and then slowly descended towards the pillar and the chair.

The light dimmed as the star fell, and through scrunched-up eyes Leaf saw that it was Lady Friday, her long, radiantly yellow wings stretched out for ten feet to either side, tip feathers ruffling as she glided down to alight on the silver chair. The radiance came from something she held in her hand, the same bright object she'd held before when leading the sleepers to the hospital pool.

The twelve sleepers raised their arms as Lady Friday settled on the chair. Leaf heard Harrison suck in air and hold it with a kind of choking noise, and she felt her own breath catch. Lady Friday languidly lifted the shining object in her hand and the light from it dimmed, then suddenly flashed, lighting up everything in the crater as if it were a giant camera flash. In that instant, the lake turned silver, like reflective glass, as did the dome above.

It felt like time stopped. Leaf was motionless, held in that light, as if caught in a still photograph. Nothing moved and she could hear no sound, not even her own beating heart. Then, very slowly, in the slowest of slow motions, she saw something coming out of the mouths and eyes of the sleepers. Tendrils of many colors, twining and twisting as they stretched across the water to the bright star in Friday's hand.

It was as if the Trustee was drawing colored threads out of their bodies. As the tendrils reached her, the light in her hand changed, the white giving way to a rainbow cluster of red, blue, green, and violet.

Then the tendrils snapped off at the sleepers' end and the trailing pieces whipped and curled as they crossed the lake into Friday's hand. The sleepers slowly crumpled to the ground, so slowly that Leaf felt as if it took seconds for them to fall.

Friday raised the glowing rainbow concoction to her mouth, tipped her head back, and drank it down. Most of the brilliant, multicolored threads went in, but she was a careless drinker and some short fragments fell and splashed on the rock before trickling down to the lake.

As Friday drank, the world returned to its normal state. Leaf heard her heartbeat come back, felt her breath rush in through nose and mouth, saw the purple sunlight wash down through the dome.

Lady Friday flexed her wings and launched into the air. Her cohorts descended to lift the chair by its straps.

"What did she do?" asked Leaf, very quietly. The sleepers were lying on the stone. Whether they still lived or not, they were still.

"She experienced them," said Harrison. His tone was flat and hollow as if he too was shocked by what he had seen, though he had seen it many times before. "Absorbed their lives, their memories and experience. The best parts, that's what she wants. To feel how they lived, how they loved, all their excitements, triumphs, and joys."

"What happens to the sleepers after . . . afterward?"

"They never really wake up," whispered Harrison. "They used to be returned to Earth. Now, with so many, I don't know . . . oh, no! She's coming over here. . . ."

Harrison bowed his head and knelt down. Leaf stood up and tried to look at the Trustee who was flying towards her, but once again the object in Lady Friday's hand was shining, and it was too bright. Leaf had to look down and then shield her eyes with her hand as Lady Friday landed in front of her, the rush of air from her wings cool on Leaf's face.

"So, you're the small troublemaker who foiled Saturday's Cocigrue," said Lady Friday. Her voice was soft but very penetrating, and it demanded attention. "Leaf, friend of the so-called Rightful Heir, this Arthur Penhaligon. How kind of you to visit."

Chapter Ten

"The wight looked askance at me," said Ugham, referring to his brief conversation with Saturday's Dusk. "I hazard he feared some ploy or contrivance, and it is certain he is wary of your power. He has agreed to wait upon you, Lord Arthur, at the appointed half-hour — yet I misdoubt it is an honest answer. More likely he awaits the arrival of more doughty warriors before ordering the assault."

"Like more of whatever was making that noise before," said Fred with a shudder.

"I just hope the Fetchers — or something worse — aren't watching the canal side," said Arthur. He pushed the shutters open wide and shivered as the wind blew in, spraying him with wet snow. "Wait till I'm down safe, then follow me one at a time."

"Hey!" Suzy protested. "I should go first, so when you fall in the canal I can get you out."

"Or me," said Fred. "I should go first. You're too important."

"I'm going first," said Arthur. "Remember what Sergeant Helve said about leading. Follow me!"

With that shout, he leaped across the gap between the window and the huge wheel, timing it so he would land on the spoke as it was almost level with the building. But he was a second off, and the ice-sheathed spoke was already tilting down. Arthur landed on it but he immediately started to slide, his fingers clutching frantically at the frozen timber as his legs went over the far side. The canal side.

His fingers slipped, unable to get a hold. Arthur swung his legs as he fell and managed to get his knee back on the spoke. Then with an effort that felt as if he might have wrenched every muscle he possessed, he hurled himself up, slithering across the spoke to the other side just in time to half-roll and half-fall off onto the snowy bank of the canal. Behind him the lower end of the spoke he'd been on entered the water with the crackle of broken ice and a threatening gurgle.

Arthur wanted to lie in the snow, no matter how cold and wet it was, but he knew he couldn't. He forced himself up and looked around to make sure there was no danger of attack. When he was sure no Fetchers or anything worse were nearby, he looked back up at the turning wheel.

Suzy was already on it, sliding down the descending spoke like a surfer down a wave. She jumped across to the shore with perfect timing, sending a spray of snow over Arthur as she touched down.

"That was fun!" she declared. Arthur scowled at her and scraped some snow off himself while he waited for Fred or Ugham to come down next.

It was Fred, who while lacking Suzy's style nevertheless did a workmanlike job of riding the spoke down on all fours, jumping like a dog at the end to land in a crouch near Suzy and Arthur.

Ugham chose an entirely different method, benefiting from having observed the others. He jumped with a dagger in his hand, thrusting it into the timber to give himself a secure handhold. He used that hold to position himself square in the middle of the spoke, then worked the dagger free, slid down to the wheel's inner rim, stood up, and stepped off onto the canal side as easily as Arthur might have stepped off an escalator back home.

"Let's go!" declared Arthur. He waved his hand and pointed west along the canal before pushing through the waist-high snow. He only went a few paces before Ugham overtook him.

"It were best I forge a path," said Ugham. Lowering his charged spear to the snow ahead, he twisted the bronze grip to activate it. The spear point glowed with sudden heat, the snow melting away to create a channel that Ugham widened by the simple method of pushing through. The three children followed in his wake, their way made much easier.

"It's a lot faster," said Arthur. "But we're leaving a completely obvious trail, not to mention the light."

"We'd leave a trail anyway," said Fred. "It's not snowing enough to cover any tracks."

"Uggie's keeping the spear point down," added Suzy. "Not that much light is showing."

"It's the only light around, though," said Arthur, glancing about. Strangely, it didn't seem any darker than it had been when he'd first looked out from the tower. He felt much colder, though, chilled through to his bones despite the heavy aprons he wore, and every few minutes a shiver would pass through him that he couldn't suppress. "But I guess we haven't got a choice. We need to find this Paper Pusher wharf quickly. I hope they've got somewhere we can shelter for the night."

"I don't think there's going to be a night," said Fred as he stopped for a moment to squint up at the snow-clouded sky. "I reckon the sun's stuck again. There won't be no morning either, though. It'll stay like this till someone fixes it."

"Great," muttered Suzy. "Perpetual twilight and freezing snow. I thought the Lower House was managed badly enough. . . ."

"It's not that bad," said Fred. "It's nice enough inside the workshops or the town."

"I bet," said Suzy. "Freezing out here, though, ain't it?"

"We'd better be quiet," ordered Arthur. It *was* freezing, and he was already greatly tempted to use the Key to warm himself . . . and the others, though they were probably better able to cope, being less mortal than himself. If they didn't find shelter, he would have to use the Key.

They slogged on through the snow in silence. As Fred had predicted, the sky grew no darker, a dim twilight prevailing. The weather remained much the same too, with scattered showers of snow that never really got started properly but also never really stopped.

After they had gone at least a mile, Arthur called a brief halt. He was very tired, mostly from the cold. The four of them huddled together around Ugham's spear point, warming their hands. Arthur could barely feel the top joints of his fingers, and his nose and cheekbones didn't feel much better.

"You need a hat, Arthur," said Suzy. She took off her own New Nithling–issue fur hat and pulled it down on Arthur's head before he could protest. Then as he feebly tried to lift it off, she whipped a handkerchief out of her sleeve and tied it over her head and ears.

"I can't take your hat," said Arthur, but Suzy skipped away as he tried to hand it back. Recognizing the futility of trying to get her to do something she didn't want to do, Arthur put the hat back on. He had to admit he immediately felt warmer. He remembered reading somewhere that people lost most of their heat through their head and kicked himself for not thinking of it before. He couldn't afford to make simple mistakes like forgetting to wear a hat.

Any more *simple mistakes,* Arthur thought.

"How far is this wharf?" asked Suzy.

"I'm not sure," Arthur confessed. "Half a parsang, whatever that is. Do you know, Fred?"

"I've never gone far from Letterer's Lark, but I don't think a half parsang is that far," said Fred. "I've seen the canal, but never a wharf. The Paper Pushers don't have a good reputation, though."

"I don't care about their reputation, so long as they have a fire," said Suzy.

Arthur nodded. He knew that if he kept talking, his teeth would chatter, and he didn't want to show the others how cold he really was. Instead he stood up and pointed west. Ugham immediately rose and started out again, once more melting the snow. Arthur followed, with Suzy close behind and Fred bringing up the rear.

They hadn't gone very far when Ugham stopped and turned back to face the others.

"Something ahead," he whispered. "Lying in the snow."

"Spread out," Arthur whispered back. He drew the Key, and for the first time he heard it make a slight humming noise as it transformed into its sword shape. If it had been a human noise it might have been something like a soft, expectant *aaahhh*. Whatever it meant, Arthur didn't like it, but he had to ignore it for the moment. He waved the sword forward, and the quartet advanced.

The something in the snow turned out to be the bodies of two Denizens, who were lying almost on top of each other. Two shabby, short Denizens who had huge holes where their hearts used to be. Blue blood was frozen all over their long coats, which were made of paper and, though different in detail, were of the same design, both being a patchwork of paper records, neatly sewn together with yellow thread.

"They're Paper Pushers," said Fred. "They wear clothes made of printed papers, in case they fall in the canal. The textually charged water repels and moves text, you see —"

"I know about that," interrupted Arthur. He looked around nervously, the cold and his weariness momentarily forgotten. "What I want to know is what could have done that to both of them? I mean they're dead. I thought

Denizens could survive all kinds of things that would kill mortals."

Ugham walked around the corpses, then bent down to sniff around their wounds.

"They were slain in the blink of an eye, sliced through as readily as I have parted the snow, and there is the stench of Nothing upon them. Betide these unfortunates were slain by a sorcerous weapon. Something akin to the sword you bear, Lord Arthur."

"What?!" exclaimed Arthur. "A Key?"

"Something most sorcerous," said Ugham. "No mere steel, nor even the weapons of your Army or mine own charged spear could spit two Denizens in a single thrust. Nor make a wound a full handspan wide."

He held up his left hand and spread his seven fingers to illustrate the point, before adding, "Whoever did this would be a foe to face indeed."

"Saturday herself, maybe," said Arthur nervously. "I don't think her Dusk could do that. He would have skewered me down in the Pit ages ago if he had that kind of weapon."

"Nah," said Suzy. "Saturday wouldn't come here herself. This is Friday's neck of the woods. They have that agreement, remember?"

"Lady Friday has abdicated," replied Arthur. He was

looking all around, peering out into the twilit snowscape. "Or so she said in her message. I guess all the usual restrictions on the other Trustees are off. Though I suppose. . . ."

"What?" asked Suzy.

"Maybe Friday killed these two," said Arthur. "Oh, I don't know! I'm too cold and tired to think straight. Let's find the wharf — but be careful."

For once Suzy didn't comment. She just nodded, as did Fred. Ugham's answer was to stride off again, this time choosing not to activate his spear, instead just pushing through the snow and making a path with his body.

The wharf was soon in sight, a dark rectangular bulk lacking all detail in the twilight. It could be a low, long hill for all Arthur could tell, but as they drew closer, Arthur saw that while the wharf itself was a simple wooden pier that thrust out fifty or sixty feet into the canal, its construction was obscured by the sheer bulk of ribbon-tied papers, stone tablets, papyrus bundles, stacks of hides, and other written records that were piled all over it, in places up to thirty feet high. It all looked extremely shaky and likely to fall down. If anything did fall down, it would probably crush any poor unfortunates who happened to be underneath. Some of the stone tablets, in particular, were larger than Arthur himself.

The four travelers advanced warily on this huge, shabby

dump of records, but there was no sudden attack, or any indication that anyone else was around. A quick circuit of the landward end of the wharf also showed that there were no buildings, not even a hut in which they might shelter.

There was, however, a small dark opening between two towering stacks of evil-smelling cured hides that had been written on in green phosphorescent ink by an untidy scribe whose lines went all over the place.

"That looks like a passage," said Suzy. "I bet there's a cozy little den inside all this stuff. Probably down the end. That's where I'd set up."

"And as like as not, an ambuscade at the end of it," said Ugham. He handed his spear to Fred and drew his knuckle-duster knife. "Dark corners lead to dark deeds."

Before Arthur could say or do anything, Ugham disappeared into the dark, narrow way, moving in a fighting crouch. The boy hesitated for a moment. But it was not from fear, just from the cold that was slowly spreading from his numb fingers and frozen toes, all the way up into his brain.

I'm slowing down, thought Arthur. *I have to get warm or I'll die. . . .*

Except he wouldn't die, he knew. His will to survive was too strong. He'd use the Key, and he'd become a Denizen. . . .

Arthur forced himself to concentrate on the immediate future rather than on what might lay ahead. He forced his cold muscles into action and followed Ugham into the dark passage, with Suzy and Fred close behind.

After only a dozen paces, Arthur had to stop. The passage between the records was getting dark, too dark to see. He could hear Ugham moving up ahead somewhere, but the way was too twisty and difficult to navigate without being able to see.

"Have either of you got some kind of light?" whispered Arthur. Suzy was right behind him now, and Fred close behind her.

"Only the spear," Fred whispered back. "But there's too much paper to turn it on. Start a fire for sure."

"No light," said Suzy. "But I can see a bit in the dark. Not as much as the Newniths, though. The Piper made them special. They like the dark. Maybe Uggie will find a lantern and come back."

"We can't just let Ugham go ahead," said Arthur. "What if there is a Trustee at the other end? Or a top-level Denizen sorcerer?"

Suzy drew breath to answer, but whatever she was about to say was completely drowned out by the sound of a terrible, inhuman scream behind them. A scream that they immediately and instinctively recognized as a cry of rage. A vengeful sound that drove all rational thought out of the three children's heads.

The scream rose to an almost unbearable pitch, then fell away in a series of horrible grunts before starting to rise again. Arthur was already running, feeling the walls and the way ahead with his hands to find the passage. He felt Suzy crashing along behind him and Fred shouting something incomprehensible that was probably "Run!"

All of them knew the scream had come from somewhere outside the wharf. Somewhere behind them. Every instinct told them to get to the end of the wharf as fast as they could.

Whatever lay ahead, hidden under the hilly peninsula of papers, tablets, hides, and papyrus scrolls, had to be less dangerous than whatever was prowling around outside, screaming its rage at the sky.

Chapter Eleven

Arthur's headlong flight ended suddenly with an impact that sent him momentarily to his knees. But the pain of running full tilt into what felt like a giant mattress — but was probably a pile of old vellum manuscripts — helped clear his head a little. In that moment of brief respite, he clutched at the Key on his belt, and though he did not order it to do anything, as soon as his fingers closed on the cool ivory, he felt the fear dissipate. He could still hear the horrible shrieking but he wasn't driven mad by a complete and unreasonable fear.

"Hold on!" shouted Arthur. He was kicked and pushed by Suzy and Fred as they tried to get past him, still fleeing from the scream. "It's some kind of sorcery. It's just a noise!"

His words had no effect. Suzy slid by and he felt the impact of Fred's elbow as he barged past. Then he was alone in the dark and they were crashing and banging their way ahead of him.

"Stop!" yelled Arthur, but he knew they wouldn't unless he actually used the power of the Key on them.

Instead he followed them at a slower pace, keeping one hand on the Key while he held his other hand out in front of himself to feel the way.

Behind him, the screaming drew closer and then was suddenly softened by the rumble of part of the wharf's piles of paper falling over, followed by angry snorting, ripping, and shoving noises as something tried to bull its way through the now-blocked passage.

Arthur felt a different fear then, but it was a rational fear. He could keep it in bounds, while trying to go just a little bit faster without running into something and knocking himself out.

He was thinking about that when he suddenly felt his way around a corner and emerged into unexpected lantern light. A single strom lantern (as they were called in the House due to a clerical error) hung from a bamboo hatstand in the far corner of a chamber about as big as his living room back home, with ragged walls of piled-high papers, a roof made of stitched-together hides covered in the sticklike writing of some strange alphabet, and a window that was haphazardly framed by two stacks of slates and a hollow log, all of them written on.

Suzy and Fred were still trying to run away but with little success, as Ugham had caught them and was holding them under his arms. At the same time he was kicking a

Denizen who was trying to hit him with a long wooden pole that had a hook on the end. Three other Denizens were hastily climbing out through the window, and beyond them Arthur could just make out the debris-filled waters of the canal.

"Back, back, foul fiend!" chanted the Denizen with the pole, and then with a half-glance behind him, "Wait for me!"

"Who dost thou call fiend?" bellowed Ugham. He kicked the pole down and advanced on the Denizen. "The fiend is without, or so that noise would attest. But where do your fellows flee?"

The Denizen looked at his empty hands, then turned and ran. Unfortunately the marble slab that was the windowsill tilted back as he jumped and he fell back down in front of Ugham, who put one heavy foot upon his chest.

At the same time, there was an immense crash somewhere back along the wharf, and the pitch of the screeching went still higher, so high that Arthur winced and a set of four recently emptied fine porcelain teacups near the window hummed and vibrated before suddenly exploding.

Just as the cups shattered, there was a very loud splash and the screaming stopped. The sound of falling bits and pieces continued, but it still felt strangely quiet.

"The creature has fallen through these rotten boards," said Ugham, "into the canal."

He stamped his foot in emphasis and the Denizen groaned. Suzy, finding herself in the crook of Ugham's left arm, tilted her head back with a puzzled look. Fred, under the Newnith's right arm, had a similar expression.

"You can put me down, Uggie," said Suzy. "I s'pose I got ensorcerated into running away."

"It was the sound," said Fred as Ugham set the two Piper's children gently on their own feet. He shook his head as if a remnant of the scream was still lodged inside. "I had to get away from the sound. What was it anyway?"

"I don't know," said Arthur. "Hopefully it's drowning. Are you a Paper Pusher?"

This question was addressed to the Denizen who was groaning under Ugham's foot. He didn't answer, but continued to moan.

"I asked if you're a Paper Pusher," said Arthur. "I'm Arthur, the Rightful Heir to the Architect, and I need your help."

Still the Denizen didn't answer, but he stopped groaning. Then, as Ugham grunted and began to press down harder with his foot, he quickly spoke.

"I'm not saying one way or another. Maybe I is a Paper

Pusher and if I am, why then, I'd be responsible for this here wharf number seventeen, stretch twelve, and I'd be a fully paid-up Branch Secretary of the Noble and Exalted Association of Waterway Motivators, and you'd not be and you'd have no business on the canal."

"What's your name and precedence within the House then, cully?" asked Suzy.

"Peter Pirkin, Primary Paper Pusher, First Class, 65,898,756th in . . . Oh, you're a sharp one. Got me proper, didn't you?"

"Okay, Peter Pirkin Paper Pusher," said Arthur. "I really am the Rightful Heir to the Architect, and that means the Middle House as well and everything and everyone in it. I need you to help me get up to Lady Friday's Scriptorium."

"Can't," said Pirkin. "And won't."

"Why can't you?" asked Arthur. "We'll deal with *won't* in a minute."

"Can't, because the canal only goes up to the Top Shelf."

"Well, you can take us that far at least," said Arthur. "Now —"

Before he could go on, the floor under his feet suddenly shuddered, and the timbers lifted up several inches before subsiding again. This phenomenon was immediately repeated, this time with a horrible grunting, gargling sound.

"It didn't drown," said Fred.

"It's under us," said Suzy.

"Let me go!" called out Pirkin. "Let me go!"

"Where?" asked Arthur. The floor was creaking and splintering all around them.

"The raft!"

Ugham picked up Pirkin by the collar of his paper-patchwork smock and ran to the window. He looked out and immediately had to dodge a thrown bronze tablet shaped like a large piece of toast.

"A strange flat vessel does indeed lie a jump away," he reported, in between ducking or dodging thrown House records of various media.

"You have to take us too!" said Arthur to Pirkin. He jumped aside as several floorboards near him suddenly exploded into splinters. A long, extremely sharp, straight spear — or horn — of pure Nothing contained within a spiral wrap of silver wire thrust through and up at least six feet before it was withdrawn. "All of us go, or all of us stay!"

"We can't!" squealed Pirkin. "You have to be a member of the association to ride the rafts!"

"We'll join!" shouted Arthur as the Nothing horn

smashed through the floor again. This time he saw the head of the beast as well. It was a Nithling, one of the elemental kind made of pure Nothing, in this case contained within an armature or framework of silver wire. It looked like a huge crazy wire sculpture, a mad cross between a unicorn and a wild boar, but with roiling dark matter inside the wire instead of empty space.

It didn't have any eyes or any visible mouth.

"You can't just join —"

"Throw him on the raft and all of you jump!" ordered Arthur. He had the Key in his hand now, in its sword form, and as the boar-unicorn smashed through again, he struck at its horn.

It was like hitting a stone, but even though Arthur's hand was jarred by the impact, the Nithling beast felt it much more. Its horn bent from the blow, it squealed, horribly loud and high-pitched, and withdrew back under the wharf.

Arthur turned, climbed through the window after the others, and jumped to the raft below, almost missing it as it was already moving away. Six Paper Pushers were shoving with their poles, the looks on their faces indicating that they were more concerned with putting some distance between themselves and the Nithling creature than anything else, including a late addition to the crew.

The seventh Paper Pusher was Pirkin. He was picking himself up with more assistance than he probably wanted from Ugham, while Suzy and Fred stared back at the collapsing wharf and the horrible beast that was climbing up through the records to shriek after them.

Fortunately the Paper Pushers knew their business well, and a swift current picked up the raft and raced it away, propelling the odd vessel several hundred yards out into the canal, with the wharf and the beast quickly lost in the gloom.

The current of textually charged water propelled the vessel, Arthur saw, because the raft was entirely covered in writing of various kinds and was in fact made up entirely of House records. In this case, hundreds or perhaps thousands of bundles of papyrus tied together with ribbon that was itself printed on, the raft then given greater structural strength by the addition of bracing struts that were long, thin planks covered in something that must be writing, though to Arthur it looked more like random woodworm trails.

The whole raft was about the size of half a football field, though parts of it looked as if they had sunk lower than intended and were waterlogged or actually submerged. The part that held Arthur's interest, though, was a hut right in the middle. A solid-looking construction of marble tablet walls and a writing slate roof, it had a chimney with smoke coming out the top and soft yellow light attested to the presence of one or more strom lanterns.

Arthur started for this shelter immediately, this time not even trying to suppress the shivers that were emerging from somewhere inside him and making his hands and teeth shudder. Part of it was cold, and part of it was shock. He'd seen some terrible things in the House, but the boar-unicorn was one of the worst.

I hope it can't swim, thought Arthur, quickly followed by, *I hope it isn't coming after us. . . .*

"Stop," said Peter Pirkin, raising one finger in Arthur's face. "All right, you're on the raft, we'll let that go by, even if it is against both the rules and the articles of the association. But you are definitely not coming into the meeting house."

"Yes we are," said Arthur simply. He brushed some snow off his shoulder and walked on. "I'm too cold to argue."

"Cold? This isn't cold!" said Pirkin. "Why, we've been in currents so cold that only the moving text keeps the ice broken and then only long enough for the raft —"

"Stand aside, please," chattered Arthur. Pirkin had kept walking backwards in front of Arthur and now stood in front of the door to the hut — a door made from a single piece of bark with pictograms on it.

"No, I really have to draw . . . Oh, stuff it. No one cares anyway. Look at all the help I get from my fellow members of the association! It's bad enough when they won't pay their dues, but as for repelling unauthorized passengers . . ."

Pirkin gestured to the half-dozen other Paper Pushers who were watching with interest from what they hoped was a safe distance, resting on the poles they had used to push off from the canal's shallower waters. Big broad-bladed paddles lay next to them, which would make quite useful weapons, but they made no move to pick them up.

Suzy waved to them, and after a moment, four of them waved back.

"Come in, then," said Pirkin with a sigh. "You'd better get out of those wet things and put on some proper written-up clothes anyway. Never know when we might all end up in the water."

Chapter Twelve

"Are you afraid?" asked Lady Friday. She folded her wings and walked closer to Leaf, who stood completely still and felt very, very small.

"Yes," whispered Leaf. The light was still too bright for her to look up, to face Lady Friday.

"It is interesting, fear," said Friday. "There is always a lot of it in you mortals. I like a little of it, but not too much. That is why those I taste must be asleep, lest present fear overwhelm the other, older experiences. Now, do you know why I have brought you here, Leaf?"

"No."

"I do not drink from young mortals," said Friday. "Their experiences are too fresh, too slight to savor. Old mortals are best. Ah, how I enjoy a lifetime of eighty or ninety mortal years, with all the complex flavors of love and hope and sorrow and joy. If only the taste lasted longer than it does. Ah, well! You have caught me full of mortal experience and I do believe some melancholy has lingered on my palate. . . . Yes, I feel quite sad that the lives I taste are so quickly gone, and I must discipline myself not to immediately have some more. . . ."

She paused, and though Leaf could not look, she had the horrible suspicion that Friday was licking her lips.

"Now, as for you, Miss Interfering Leaf. I have brought you here because even though I have a most excellent plan to not only remove your friend Arthur but also several other major annoyances, I am not so stupid as to count on its success. My spies tell me Arthur is most attached to his friends, that he would do anything to help them. So you will serve as bait for a trap, or as a negotiating point, or a hostage, or something equally useful should the occasion arise. Just do as you are told and stay out of the way."

"What if I don't?" said Leaf, but again it didn't come out as defiant. It sounded pathetic and hopeless.

"You are also not stupid, I think," said Friday. "As I hold you to use against Arthur, I hold someone to use against you. Do I not?"

Leaf froze, unable to think of any response to that.

"Do I not?" snapped Friday. "Some blood relation, I think. Aunt Orange or Apple or some such fruity name."

"Mango," whispered Leaf. "Don't . . . please don't experience her."

I'm begging, she thought, some part of her unable to

believe the situation she was in. *I'm begging for Mango's life, or something close to it.*

"Oh, I can still feel the poignancy of it!" declared Friday. "The emotion is lasting longer! I almost feel like a mortal and it must be at least a minute. . . . No . . . it's fading. . . . Axilrad, I must have another batch. . . . No . . . too soon . . . I'll run out . . . perhaps some other distraction . . ."

Leaf heard the Trustee's wings unfurl and she threw herself forward, onto the hard stone.

"Please! Don't do anything to Aunt Mango!"

"Your mango shall be the last fruit I taste," called out Friday with a clear, carrying laugh, and then with a single, powerful beat of her wings, she leaped back up into the air.

Leaf stayed facedown, trying not to sob, her hand unconsciously going to the Mariner's medallion, her fingers clutching it so hard they turned almost as white as the whalebone disc.

She lay there for at least a minute, letting the fear slowly ebb away, to be equally slowly replaced by her natural courage and determination. Now that Lady Friday had gone, she could think again, no longer struck with a feeling that had been as close to blind panic as she'd ever experienced.

So long as Friday's not in front of me I can be brave,

thought Leaf. She bit back a sob. *That's better than being a total coward, I guess. I just have to stay out of her way. . . .*

"I told you," said Harrison. "Guess you'll help me now, won't you?"

Leaf didn't answer. She slowly stood up and looked over at the balcony on the crater rim where Lady Friday and her attendants were alighting. She watched them go inside, ignoring Harrison.

If I give in now, she'll just experience Aunt Mango anyway, thought Leaf. *Giving in never works . . . and I can't let her use me against Arthur. . . .*

"I said you'd better help me now," said Harrison again, stepping around so he was in front of her and she couldn't ignore him.

"Why?" asked Leaf. "She won't keep her word. Besides, Arthur will sort her out before too long. You'd do better to help me."

"What?" asked Harrison weakly. "But you've seen Her, the power of the Key. . . ."

"You'd better decide whose side you're on," said Leaf. "You said you wanted to get back to Earth, didn't you?"

"Yes . . ."

"Do you reckon Lady Friday will ever let you go?"

"No . . ."

"Then help me!" urged Leaf. "Is there a telephone anywhere here that connects with the House?"

"I don't . . ." replied Harrison. He looked around, to check if any Denizens were in earshot, but he and Leaf were alone in the crater, save for the fallen sleepers who lined the shore.

"I don't know. . . ." he continued. "I'd have to ask a Denizen. But they'd never tell me. It's pointless anyway. Just help me work and we'll both stay out of trouble."

"Staying out of trouble won't get you back to Earth," said Leaf. "Or help anyone else. I'm frightened by Friday too, but we have to do *something*!"

"I can't," whispered Harrison. "I . . . I haven't got the guts. Not anymore."

"Cover for me, then," said Leaf. "Give me some job that'll let me wander around carrying something."

She didn't mention that this was a trick she'd learned from her friend the Ship's Boy Albert, who'd been killed by Feverfew. *Skiving,* he'd called it. The trick was to find something that looked like it needed to be delivered somewhere else on the ship and then you could walk around for ages with it before someone in authority noticed and took action. Denizens in particular were susceptible to this ruse, as they couldn't imagine someone inventing a task for themselves.

"But if you're caught somewhere you shouldn't be, they'll blame me!"

"If you won't help, then you're as bad as She is," said Leaf. "You'll be with the enemy when Arthur gets here."

"He will come? You're sure? Is he really ten feet tall?"

"He will come," said Leaf with a conviction she was far from feeling. "He's . . . he's not quite *that* tall, but he is . . . um . . . well, he's beaten four Trustees already."

"I guess you could go get pillowcases from the linen store," said Harrison. He was weakening, Leaf could tell. "But that won't help you find a phone. Like I said, you'd have to ask a Denizen. . . ."

"Yes," said Leaf. "I have an idea about who to ask. Where is the linen store?"

Harrison didn't answer; instead, his face twisted up in indecision.

"Remember, helping me is helping Arthur, and he's your only chance of ever getting away from here," said Leaf. "It's now or never."

"I'll do it. . . ." said Harrison. "I mean, okay! I'll do it. Come on — I'll show you the way to the linen store. It's at Circle Three, Twenty-five Past."

"What about them?" asked Leaf quietly, pointing to the quiet bodies on the shore.

"Martine takes them from here," said Harrison. "She'll come out when the sun goes down."

"Who's Martine? A Denizen?"

"No, she's human too. She's been here longer than me. Crazy as a loon, though. She only works nights. Not that night here is anything like home. There's three moons and they're big . . . and they change color."

"Maybe she's worth talking to," said Leaf. "Where would I find her?"

"Circle Six, Half-Past," muttered Harrison. He started walking back to the door where they'd entered the crater. "But she *is* crazy. Come on!"

Leaf followed him, but not without a glance back at the sleepers.

"Also, I need a drink. Have you got human food and, drink, and uh, a toilet I can use? And tea?"

"I get basic food and there are four restroom facilities for us mortals throughout the establishment," said Harrison. "But I don't have any tea. The Denizens love the stuff and they keep it for themselves. I don't have any coffee either, so you'll have to make do with water."

"Oh, I don't want the tea to drink myself," said Leaf. "I was thinking about using it to trade with a Denizen. I'll have to think of something else."

Just after she spoke, a thought did occur to her and she

bent down and picked up a small stone, one of the few that lay around the smooth floor of the crater.

"By the way, do you know where that Denizen Feorin hangs out?" Leaf asked.

"There aren't many Denizens here," said Harrison. "Maybe fifty altogether. Most are up on Circle Ten from Ten to Noon to Ten Past. I guess they have rooms there. They supposedly patrol around as well, but I don't often see them on my rounds — which reminds me, I'll have to get started again soon. Got to keep everyone turned. . . ."

He sighed and bent his head, and the small spring in his step that had come on when he agreed to help Leaf disappeared, giving way to his usual depressed shuffle. Leaf followed silently, her head full of plans and schemes, most of which she had to admit were totally impractical. She kept coming back to just three basic aims, but was entirely unsure how she might achieve them.

First, find a telephone to the House and call Arthur. Second, find Aunt Mango and get her away from wherever she is. Three, hide out with Mango somewhere until help comes.

Actually, there were four basic aims, Leaf thought, and the fourth was perhaps the most strident in her mind.

Keep away from Lady Friday.

As Harrison had predicted, they met no one on the way

to the linen store. This was a chamber almost identical to the room where Leaf had found the Skinless Boy's pocket. It brought back unpleasant memories and also made her think, because the linen was all branded with the name of the same laundry service that served East Area Hospital.

"All this stuff gets washed back on Earth, right? Not here."

"I guess so," said Harrison. "I dump the dirty sheets and stuff in a chute and get the fresh linen here. . . ."

"So someone must take it back and forth," said Leaf. "There must be a way between here and Lady Friday's hospital back on Earth."

"If there is, you need to have her power to use it," said Harrison.

Leaf shook her head.

"No way Lady Friday takes the dirty laundry to Earth and carries back a load of fresh sheets herself! So there must be a way . . . but maybe it's some kind of sorcery. It's worth checking out, though."

"I have to get back to the people stores . . . I mean wards," said Harrison nervously. He was backsliding already. "Axilrad might come looking. Don't stay away too long. You'd better come and help me fairly soon, otherwise —"

"You go, then," said Leaf. "I'll find you when I need you."

"Don't do . . . well, don't. . . ." Harrison's voice trailed off. He looked at the floor, scuffed his feet, and left.

Leaf looked around the linen store till she found a loose bolt in one of the metal shelves. She pulled it out and used it to scratch some invented letters onto the stone from the crater, in an effort to make it look interesting and strange. Perhaps even *sorcerous*. . . .

At the same time, she practiced a rhythmic, barking cough.

"*Ah-woof, ah-woof, ah-woof.*"

Chapter Thirteen

Arthur stretched out his arms and drew his hands into the sleeves of his new paper-patchwork coat, so Pirkin could cut the cuffs to the right length. The Denizen was using a huge, old pair of bronze scissors, which should have made Arthur nervous, but he was feeling quite relaxed. It was very warm inside the hut on the raft, thanks to a fridge-sized porcelain stove that was sitting on a ten-by-ten-foot slab of red stone deeply chiseled with huge incomprehensible letters. There was no fire visible through the stove's smoky quartz door, nor had Arthur seen it fed with any fuel, but there had been smoke outside.

New, dry clothes were also a good thing. Arthur, like the others, was now completely dressed (from underclothes up) in garments made from paper or parchment or soft hide, all with lines and lines of writing. He'd expected the clothes to be itchy or uncomfortable, especially the paper coat, but they were surprisingly soft and comfortable. He'd also thought they'd be no use outside in the wet snow, but Pirkin had explained that they would shed water. It was one of the Paper Pushers' few unique powers, to make clothes that would survive work on the canal and be proof against both textually charged water and the normal kind.

Arthur was also pleased because the raft was moving along the canal at quite a high speed, perhaps twenty miles an hour, fast enough to generate quite a wash behind it. So he was moving towards his objective — if indeed Lady Friday's Scriptorium was his objective. He was having some thoughts about the situation and what he should do, and was weighing whether he should discuss matters with Suzy and Fred.

They are my friends, he thought. *But they are also bound to serve the Piper. Ugham is a good bloke, but ultimately he has to serve the Piper too. If we get to the Key, Ugham would have to try to take it for the Piper . . . or rather, call the Piper in, since he wouldn't be able to take it himself. I wonder if he has some means of contacting the Piper. . . .*

Pirkin finished cutting the sleeves and took up a long needle and some red thread, swiftly hemming the cuffs to finish the process. Arthur was the last to be outfitted, as he had ordered, unconsciously following the ethos of the Army of the Architect, that an officer must look after his or her soldiers first. Suzy and Fred, already resplendent in their typographical coats, had gone outside to make sure the boar-unicorn Nithling was not somehow pursuing them, Ugham following them like a large and faithful hound shepherding some toddlers. The Newnith had been reluctant to change his uniform, but had complied when Pirkin explained that the textually charged currents and other sorceries in the canal would actively try to drown anyone not wearing the correct clothing, as made by the Paper Pushers.

The Piper and Saturday will go for the Scriptorium, thought Arthur. *One of them will almost certainly get there before I do, and they will also probably fight over it and try to stop each other. But if I can find Part Five of the Will, it doesn't matter who has the Fifth Key; the Will can help me get it. Particularly since I don't trust Lady Friday anyway. So I should try to find the Will first. Though it might also be in the Scriptorium . . . I wish Dr. Scamandros were here to do that spell with the gold leaf. . . .*

"Cup of hot water?" asked Pirkin, interrupting Arthur's reverie. "We haven't got any tea. Not anymore. We had some on the wharf, but . . ."

"Sure." Though Arthur was now quite warm, a cup of hot anything would be welcome. It might help banish the memory of the cold — and would help if he had to go outside, where it was still snowing. "Are the other Paper Pushers coming in? They don't need to do any poling now, do they?"

"We're in the up seven-six current now, and the canal is a full twenty fathoms deep," said Pirkin. He was quite agreeable now that he had given up trying to prevent Arthur and the others from boarding the raft. "But someone has to watch the raft, make sure nothing falls off or sinks, to upset the trim. Besides, they're not so used to strangers, being as how they're only ordinary members of the association and not Branch Secretary like I am."

Arthur gratefully took the steaming enamel cup he was offered.

"Thanks. So we're in an up-current? How long will it take to get to the Middle of the Middle? And can we keep going from there to the Top Shelf?"

"We'll reach the Lower Sky by morning," said Pirkin. "Then it depends how long to get through the skylock —"

"The Lower Sky? Skylock?" asked Arthur. "What do you mean? I thought the Middle House was all one big mountain."

"It is and it isn't," said Pirkin. He took a swig of his hot water. "Ah, that's the stuff. Nearly as good as tea, leastways if you haven't got any tea. Where was I? Oh, the Lower Sky. There's a sky above the Flat, that's the Lower Sky. And there's a sky between the Middle of the Middle and the Top Shelf, that's the Middle Sky. And then there's a sky right up top, I suppose. Least there's clouds and suns and suchlike up above the Top Shelf. Top Sky, that would be."

"And the skylock?"

"Where the canal goes through," said Pirkin. "Big gate that slides across. Oh, it's a right pain to open, I tell you. Needs a hundred ordinary members of the association on the windlass and a couple of Branch Secretaries, at least, to do the counting. Risky business too. Long way to fall if you step off the canal side."

"So how long will it take to get through?"

"Depends, don't it?" said Pirkin, with a shrug that spilled hot water on himself. He didn't seem to notice, though it would have badly scalded a human. "If there's enough rafts queued on either side, it might already be open, or we can open it fast-like."

"And once we're in the Middle of the Middle, how long to get through there and on to the Top Shelf?" asked Arthur.

"Couple of days," said Pirkin. "Depends on cargo. Got to stop at Burinberg and pick up. Unless everything's gone to pieces."

"Gone to pieces? How exactly?"

Pirkin looked at Arthur with surprise.

"Well, you're part of it, aren't you? Oddkin's raft

dropped us some letters when he passed. . . . Where are they now?"

He fished around in his pockets, drawing out numerous folded papers, till he found what he was looking for and handed them to Arthur.

"First one said Lady Friday's nicked off somewhere and that everyone who wants to should take a holiday and experiencing's allowed," said Pirkin. "Second one says Lady Friday's handed over to Superior Saturday, work must go on as usual, experiencing's not allowed, obey Saturday's officers and so on and so forth."

Arthur quickly scanned the two letters, which had the colorful seals of the relevant Trustee. The first did indeed confirm that Lady Friday was going away, but it did not specifically mention abdication or handing over the Key or her authority in the Middle House.

The second, from Superior Saturday, was much more explicit. Arthur read it in full.

To all Denizens of authority in the Middle House, Greeting

The Lady Friday, Former Trustee of the Architect, has abdicated and resigned from all authority within the Middle House. Her place has been assumed by Lady Saturday, Superior Sorcerer of the Upper House.

All Denizens in the Middle House must acknowledge the authority of Superior Saturday and her officers.

You are instructed to follow the orders of any of Superior Saturday's officers, such orders to take precedence over any standing orders, former orders, traditions, commonplace actions, rituals, regular tasks, or anything else that may conflict with said orders or instructions.

All Denizens of the Middle House will continue with their regular work. The practice known as "experiencing" is forbidden, and the possession of a "mortal experience" is decreed to be a crime, punishable to the utmost degree by any officer of the Upper House.

All Denizens of the Middle House are to cooperate with the officers, troops, and auxiliaries of the Upper House. Some auxiliaries may appear to be Nithlings. They are not Nithlings as such, but auxiliaries in the service of the Upper House.

All Denizens of the Middle House must immediately report to the nearest officer from the Upper House if they should observe, notice, hear, or become cognizant of any information concerning the whereabouts or intentions of the dangerous outlaw Arthur Penhaligon, self-styled Rightful Heir to something or other.

All Denizens of the Middle House must immediately report to the nearest officer from the Upper House if they should observe, notice, hear, or become cognizant of any information concerning the whereabouts or intentions of the rebel known as the Piper, or the malcontent known as the Mariner (aka "the Captain").

All Piper's children in the Middle House are, as of now, outlawed and must be destroyed. Loyal Denizens of the Middle House are called upon to attack Piper's children whenever and wherever they are seen. Evidence in the form of their detached heads should be retained in suitable sacks for presentation to officers of the Upper House.

All creatures known as Raised Rats are, as of now, outlawed and must be destroyed. Loyal Denizens of the Middle House are called upon to attack Raised Rats whenever and wherever they are seen. Evidence in the form of their detached tails should be retained in suitable sacks for presentation to officers of the Upper House.

All and any possessions of any captured Raised Rat or Piper's Child must also be retained in separate labelled stacks. Should any Raised Rat or Piper's Child be found to be in possession of a letter or any document, said document must be delivered with utmost haste to any officer of the Upper House.

By order of Lady Saturday, Superior Sorcerer of the Upper House, with tacit approval of Lord Sunday

Arthur frowned. The letter had the seal of Lady Saturday, a gold disc attached by rainbow-hued wax that constantly changed color . . . but it did not have Sunday's seal. And what did "tacit" mean?

I've got to find out more about Lord Sunday, thought

Arthur. He'd been thinking this for some time. *All the things that are done against me seem to be organized by Saturday, and Sunday is just in the background . . . or is he?*

He dismissed the thought for the moment. He had to concentrate on what was in front of him right now.

"Have you read *all* of this second letter?" Arthur asked Pirkin cautiously. His hand fell to the Fourth Key at his side. He hadn't put his belt back on, but he'd made sure it was never out of reach.

"I read 'em both," said Pirkin. "But like Oddkin said, it's just a load of old jetsam. Kill Piper's children? Kill Raised Rats? That's not something the association would stand for, I tell you. That Saturday ain't got no rights here. She can do whatever she wants in the Upper House, I suppose, but no one here is going to do stupid stuff just because she says so."

He paused to take another sip of his hot water, then added, "Or almost nobody. I s'pose those toffee-noses up on the Top Shelf might want to look good. They're always going on about how close they are to the Upper House anyhow. 'Top of the Middle just means bottom of the Upper' they like to say. Most of 'em failed school there, I reckon. They should stick to fixing up records like they're supposed to."

"I hope you're right," said Arthur. He started to lift his

cup but had to grab it with both hands as the raft suddenly lurched and the floor tilted sharply, making his chair slide back to the wall. "What's happening?!"

"Started up the rise, haven't we," said Pirkin. He put down his cup and moved to the door. "Not before time too. About ten hours' climb to the Skylock and then we should see some sunshine in the Middle. Their weather isn't broken. I'd best see we're in the fastest current."

As Pirkin left the hut, Arthur settled back in his chair. The floor of the raft was now tilted up at about twenty degrees, which both looked and felt quite strange, but Pirkin had not been concerned so Arthur figured he would try not to be as well.

He had just taken his long-delayed sip when the door opened and Suzy and Fred burst in, accompanied by a cold gust of wind and some flying snow. They advanced cautiously to the stove, the canted floor giving them some trouble, and sat down with their backs to the stove, facing Arthur.

"No sign of the pig thing," said Suzy. "But Uggie's keeping watch."

"Never thought I'd go for a ride on a Paper Pusher's raft," said Fred. "Particularly not when I was up for another ninety-nine years of service in the Army before I could even get back to Letterer's Lark."

"Still want to be a General, Fred?" asked Arthur.

Fred shook his head slowly and fingered the line of writing around his neck.

"In whose army?" he said. "I don't reckon Marshal Noon or anyone would trust me now."

"I'm sure that can be removed," said Arthur. "Dr. Scamandros, or Dame Primus —"

"Can *you* do it now?" asked Suzy. "I just can't stand *having* to obey the —"

"Suzy! Stop!" both Fred and Arthur interrupted, but it was too late.

"— the Piper," finished Suzy and as the word left her mouth, the line on her throat gave out a low, whistling hum and both boys saw it suddenly contract on Suzy's throat.

Suzy coughed once and fell to the floor, sliding down to Arthur's feet. Her face went bright red and she scratched desperately at her neck, the writing there stark white against the red, irritated skin.

"Arthur!" shouted Fred. "Do something!"

Arthur hesitated, but only for a second. He didn't really have a choice. He drew the baton that was the Fourth Key and held it against Suzy's throat as she thrashed at his feet.

"Release Suzy from the Piper's bonds," he said quietly. A faint glow of green light appeared around the baton, and a similar glow surrounded Suzy's throat. It grew brighter for an instant, bright as an emerald in the sun, then disappeared, taking with it the line of type that forced Suzy to the Piper's service.

As Suzy took in a deep, racking breath, Arthur stood up and held the baton to Fred's throat, repeating the process.

It only took a few seconds to release both of them. Arthur sat back down, put the baton on his lap, and raised his empty hand. The crocodile ring on his finger caught the light, glinting in almost equal parts silver and gold. Arthur had to look at it more closely to see that, as he had expected, the gold had crept farther past the fifth line.

"You did that on purpose, didn't you, Suzy?" he said bitterly. "To make me use the Key."

"I didn't really mean to, Arthur," said Suzy, though her voice lacked conviction. "It just came out!"

"Sure," said Arthur. He shook his head in exasperation.

"Thanks, though," said Suzy. She punched Arthur lightly on the shoulder, but he did not react and she stepped back.

"Yes, thank you, Arthur," said Fred. "It was more than a bit of a worry, you know, not knowing if it was going to choke me sometime. Or cut my head off."

Arthur didn't answer. He was furious with Suzy for

forcing him to use the Key, but he was also angry with himself for being furious, because it felt so mean not to help his friends when they needed it, just to save himself from becoming a Denizen.

The three of them sat in silence for a few minutes, neither Suzy nor Fred looking up at Arthur. He, in turn, looked down and turned the crocodile ring on his finger so that only the silver side showed. Then he turned it again, back to the gold, and kept on turning, till at last he sighed and looked up.

"What's Ugham going to do?" asked Arthur.

"I think he'll be all right," said Fred. "The Newniths are funny. The ones we were with kept talking about gardening. They're good soldiers, but they don't like soldiering, I reckon. They owe the Piper because he made them, but they don't volunteer to do anything."

"Uggie's said he'll only do what he was ordered to do," said Suzy. "Look after us. 'Course, if he gets new orders, that's different."

"We'll have to be careful," said Arthur.

"Look on the bright side, Arthur," said Suzy. "Now —"

"What bright side?" interrupted Arthur crossly. "You just don't take anything seriously, Suzy!"

"She really didn't mean to make you use the Key,

Arthur," said Fred cautiously. "Maybe you should say sorry, Suzy."

"Sorry," muttered Suzy.

Arthur let out an exasperated sigh, and with it, most of his anger. He never could stay angry with Suzy, even though he knew she had almost gotten herself killed just then on purpose, to make him use his power and free her from the Piper's compulsion.

"Oh, forget it!" he said. "Okay! Tell me what the bright side is."

"Now you can tell us what we're going to do so you can get the Key and fix Friday for good and proper!"

"Yes!" said Fred, his face brightening. "What's the plan?"

Arthur frowned again, this time in thought, not anger.

"You do have a plan, don't you?" asked Fred.

"Yes," admitted Arthur. "But I'm not sure it's a very good one. We'll need to find a sorcerer, for a start. Or somehow get in touch with Dr. Scamandros. Or I suppose we might be able to find out what we need to know some other way. Or —"

"How about you tell us the plan?" said Suzy. "Before the others come back in? Between Fred and me, we can probably fix it up."

"Thanks!" said Arthur, not without sarcasm. "It is

pretty basic. First, the Piper and Saturday will both go for Lady Friday's Scriptorium to try to seize the Key. They'll expect me to do the same, and I guess that's what Friday would predict I'd do. But I think I'll try to find the Fifth Part of the Will first, which may or may not be in the Scriptorium but probably is in the Middle House. And I have a way to find the Will. At least I think I do, if I can get a sorcerer to do a simple spell. If there are any sorcerers in the Middle House. . . ."

"Sorcerers?" asked Fred. "Depends on what kind of sorcery. There's heaps of Denizens who use sorcery up in the Top Shelf. Most of the High Guild, though they're not exactly what you'd call full sorcerers, like that Dr. Scamandros. Binding and Restoration, that's mostly sorcery anyway. What do you want one of them to do?"

Arthur was about to answer when the door flung open and Pirkin leaned in, his face framed by a flurry of snow. An icicle fell off his nose and bounced on the stone floor.

"All hands on deck!" he said. "There's some kind of battle going on above us, up under the sky!"

Chapter Fourteen

It was cold out on deck, colder than it had been before, but it was no longer snowing. The raft, traveling up the canal at a sharp angle, was already breaking through the low clouds, and the sky around them was clear and much lighter, though it did grow darker again overhead. Arthur could see a slice of the sun on the far horizon, where it had presumably stuck, its light falling in a tight band that did not extend to the top of the canal.

There were some other lights in the darkness above, twinkling faux stars on the underside of the intermediate roof. Somewhere unseen up there was the skylock through which the canal would pass.

As Arthur stared up, he saw half a dozen new stars move swiftly across the sky, till one of them suddenly exploded into many smaller, fiery fragments that rained down in a quickly fading shower. The other five swerved away and grew fainter, till they disappeared again.

"A skirmish of the air," said Ugham. "I know not the combatants. One side is lit fair, the other stalks in darkness. Ah, the light-bearers come again!"

He pointed at a different quarter of the sky. This time more than a dozen stars were moving in an arrowhead formation towards the point where the explosion had been. The stars grew brighter as they crossed the sky, and Arthur realized that they were drawing closer to the raft, descending as well as moving horizontally.

"Who are they?" Arthur asked Pirkin.

"Dunno," answered the Paper Pusher. "I know who's waiting in the dark, though."

"So do I," breathed Fred. Arthur glanced at his friend, who was staring entranced up at the sky.

"Who?"

"Winged Servants of the Night," Fred and Pirkin said together. Pirkin had a strange catch to his voice, a melancholy that Arthur had not heard there before.

As they spoke, two of the bright stars once more exploded into sparks, which slowly drifted down before fading away.

"That'll be lit-up wing feathers falling," said Suzy. "Whatever was wearing them will have a long way to fall."

Suzy's comment made Arthur look back down and around. In the swath of light from the stuck sun, he could finally see the other side of the canal. It was at least half a mile away, but the width of the canal was not the most impressive thing about the waterway. It stretched ahead in a straight line for several miles before curving to the right, all the time climbing at a gentle ten degrees. At the curve, Arthur could see that the whole vast canal was supported on thousands of columns that disappeared down into the clouds. It looked like an impossible freeway flyover stretched up a thousand times and then flooded with water. Seeing it made him feel nervous and slightly giddy.

It was easier to look up, so Arthur did, just in time to see something come hurtling down towards them. It had been practically invisible until it fell into the sunlight, a black speck against the black sky. It fell like a stone towards the raft, and for a moment Arthur thought it was some kind of missile. But when it got to several hundred yards out he saw it was roughly human-shaped — and that it was going to miss the raft and possibly the canal as well, to plummet down to the Flat.

Then a black, crow-shaped wing spread out from its left shoulder, and, from its right, a crumpled, bent-up mess of wild feathers. Flapping madly with its single working wing, the creature corrected its course towards the raft and slowed a little, corkscrewing wildly as it fell.

It hit the raft at a speed that would have killed any mortal, bounced twice, and immediately started to get up. Arthur thought it had to be some kind of Nithling, and his hand was on the Key as he raced over to it, on the heels of

Ugham, Fred, and Suzy. Pirkin lagged behind, his head bent and his feet slow.

But it was not a Nithling. As Arthur got nearer, he saw that the creature's strange beaked head was a helmet with a long, open snout through which a Denizen's mouth could be vaguely seen. Similarly, what looked like a natural leathery hide was a full bodysuit of black armor, and the taloned, webbed hands were actually taloned, webbed gauntlets of the same black material.

It was impossible to tell if it was a male or female Denizen. It got to its knees as Arthur and the others approached, one wing crushed at its side, the other trailing behind. It tried to stand but couldn't and fell back into a crouch.

"Is it . . . this . . . a Winged Servant of the Night?" Arthur whispered to Fred as they slowed to stand in a ring around the crippled flyer, no one sure what to do next.

"Yes," said Fred. He pushed past and kneeled by the strange Denizen, his hands and fingers moving in a series of complicated signs.

The Servant seemed startled, then quickly signed back, too quickly for Fred.

"Slow down!" he said and made several emphatic finger movements.

The Servant signed again, with greater deliberation and many more pauses.

"She . . . her name is . . . ah, something like . . . Cool of the Evening Before Full Dark. She says they are fighting winged Denizens from the Upper House. I think they're called something like Clever Resters?"

"Artful Loungers," said Ugham. "Our lord has made us study all the foe we might face. They are not the most puissant of Saturday's host."

The Servant nodded.

"She can hear?" asked Arthur.

The Servant nodded again.

"Sorry," Arthur continued. "I mean, you can hear, but you don't speak, right?"

The Servant nodded again.

"I didn't know that," said Fred. "But then, I never did meet a real Servant before."

"How come you know the signs, then?" Suzy asked.

Fred coughed and looked away from the Servant and mumbled something.

"You what?" Suzy persisted.

"Thought I might grow up to be a Winged Servant." Fred's cheeks were red, and not just from the cold. "There was a book of signs I did a bit of gilding on . . . part of a manual for Middle House management. I kept it and learned how to do them."

"But Piper's children don't grow up," said Arthur, puzzled.

"I know," said Fred sadly. "It was just . . . something to pretend. I didn't want to be a gilding assistant forever. It's lucky I can still remember most of the signs I learned. It was a long time ago and someone took the book back. I've been washed between the ears many times since then."

Arthur scowled at the mention of the washing between the ears. He wanted to know more about that whole process, and why it was done. It was yet another small mystery of the House that needed sorting out, but had to be put on the backburner.

The Servant tapped Fred on the foot to make him pay attention, and her fingers spelled out a long message.

"She has to get back into the fight; she wants to know if we have extra wings," said Fred. "Any wings will do."

"We haven't got any," said Arthur. "Well, unless Pirkin has some. . . ."

"Wings is for those who don't have a canal to ride," said Pirkin. "The Association expressly forbids wings on the rafts. Why, if it wasn't for the extenuating circumstances, I'd have to ask Miss Cool of the Evening here to take her leave. . . ."

The Servant hissed and reached for a slim metal tube at her belt.

"However, given there *is* extenuations aplenty," Pirkin said hurriedly, "welcome aboard. I don't suppose one more nonmember will make any difference."

The Servant nodded and tried to get up once more. Fred and Arthur quickly helped her, but she shrugged them off and managed to keep standing alone. She raised one foot that could not bear her weight, either because it or her leg was broken. She made more signs and Fred translated.

"Her companions will come for her soon, if they win," he said. "Or the enemy. She suggests we stand away in case it is the latter. The Artful Loungers will leave us alone, as they have left the other rafts alone."

"Other rafts?" asked Pirkin. "Where?"

The Servant pointed up and again signed out a long message.

"The skylock has been captured by the enemy," passed on Fred. "It is being held open to allow the Artful Loungers to fly down from Burinberg, which was taken by Saturday's troops earlier today in a massed elevator assault.

"Um, Friday's Dawn has refused to accept Saturday's authority and has ordered all loyal Middle House Denizens to resist. Friday's Dawn and his Gilded Youths tried to hold Burinberg but have been forced to retreat to the Top

Shelf. No one knows where Friday's Noon and Dusk are, or Lady Friday.

"Let's see . . . the High Guild in the Top Shelf has not declared for either side. The Winged Servants are basically attacking Saturday's forces wherever they can till morning, since they only fly at night. Can you repeat that last bit?"

Fred watched the repeated signs carefully.

"Oh, the rafts . . . lots of them were held up by the fighting at the skylock but now they're passing through. The Loungers are too busy fighting the Servants and are ignoring the rafts. Did I get all that right, miss?"

The Servant nodded, but her head was craned back, her masked head scanning the sky above, her hand once more on the tube at her belt. It looked to Arthur like a miniature version of the firewash projectors used by the Army of the Architect . . . which would be a very nasty weapon indeed. He was determined to keep a careful eye on it.

"Why did you land here?" Arthur asked now. "Why did you think you would be safe? We're obviously not Paper Pushers."

Cool of the Evening shook her head and quickly signed a reply, without taking her gaze away from the sky.

"You smell all right," said Fred. "Saturday's Denizens

smell of . . . I don't know that sign . . . stone-smoke? Coal, maybe."

"The noses of the Servants are keen," said Ugham.

Cool of the Evening made another rapid sign.

"Flyers coming down," said Fred.

"As are their eyes," said Ugham. "I do not spy any movement."

"Could be Loungers with their wings darked," said Fred. "What do we do, Arthur? We can't just leave her —"

"Of course not!" Arthur drew the Key, the Servant hissing in surprise and shielding her eyes as the baton transformed into a silver rapier, the metal brighter than could be explained by the mere reflection of light. "Prepare to receive boarders!"

Chapter Fifteen

When she was satisfied with both her fake cough and her scratched-up stone, Leaf took an armful of pale blue pillowcases and started around the circle to the nearest stairs. A plan had formed in her head . . . or at least part of a plan. It had several defects, which she hoped to overcome on the fly, because she couldn't think of anything else she could do.

The first step was to find the Denizen called Feorin, but without Milka in attendance. Feorin might be stupid enough to fall for Leaf's intended trick, but she knew there was little chance Milka would go along with it.

Maybe I can find another stupid Denizen, thought Leaf as she trudged up the stairs to circle ten and headed around toward the noon position, where the Denizens' quarters were. As Harrison had predicted, she didn't meet anyone. The corridor was deserted and looked just like all the other corridors she'd walked inside the crater rim. If it wasn't for the numbers above the doors and the staircases, she would have sworn she was back where she originally came in.

I suppose I'll have to knock on a door. Which could lead to trouble. . . .

Uncertain about whether this was a good idea, Leaf walked the top part of the circle, trying to see if there was any clue to be found as to who might be behind the doors. But the only one that was different was the one at the noon position, which was wider and had an ornate pattern around the doorknob. Leaf thought this was probably a good one to avoid and, at random, chose to knock on the door at six past twelve.

It was opened very quickly by a Denizen who was holding a large needle and dangling gold thread in one hand and a book in the other. He looked over Leaf's head and then, seeing no one, down at her.

"What is it?"

"Uh, sorry to disturb you," said Leaf. "I've been sent to give a message to Feorin."

"Feorin? Are you sure?"

"Yes, definitely Feorin."

"Try next door," said the Denizen, pointing clockwise with the needle. "Ten past."

"Thanks," said Leaf, the door already shutting in her face. She took a deep breath and walked along to the door at ten past, hesitated for a moment, then sharply rapped on it.

The occupants were not so fast this time. Leaf could faintly hear a conversation, then footsteps. Finally the door opened to reveal Feorin, now wearing a leather apron over his sharp suit.

Leaf stepped back so she was out of the line of sight of anyone farther inside, then coughed her odd, barking cough. "Hi, Feorin," she said. "I've got something for you."

"For me?" asked Feorin. He stepped out into the corridor after her. At the same time, someone inside — almost certainly Milka — called out, "Who is it?"

"Tell her it's a messenger," whispered Leaf. She coughed again and held out the stone she'd scratched up. "And I'll give you this . . . *ah-woof* . . . coughstone."

"A messenger!" called out Feorin. He advanced on Leaf, reaching for the stone . . . but she was too quick for him and retreated, coughing again.

"You have to help me find a telephone to the House first," whispered Leaf. "Then you can have the coughstone."

"What's the message?" Milka called out from inside.

"Tell her nothing important," hissed Leaf anxiously.

"Nothing important," called out Feorin. "It's just that sleeper!"

Leaf groaned.

"Was that part of the cough?" asked Feorin.

"No," said Leaf. As she expected, Milka came out the door. She was also wearing a leather apron and was holding a glue pot.

"What is it, then?" she asked.

"What?" asked Leaf dully. Her plan had fallen apart.

"The message," said Milka impatiently. "So you are a Piper's child after all? I always said we needed some here to run messages."

"Uh, yes," said Leaf, her brain suddenly re-engaging. "That's what I'm here for. You two are supposed to take me to a telephone so I can call . . . um . . . a sorcerer in the House to order in some special items for you Denizens. This coughstone is a sample . . . only I might have used it ah . . . ah . . . *ah-woof* . . . up."

"Good!" said Feorin. Milka didn't answer, instead reaching over to take the stone.

Leaf held her breath as the Denizen examined it and popped it in her mouth. It lodged in her throat for a few seconds and her breath caught, a hideous whistle emerging from her mouth. Then it was gone, into her stomach.

"A whistle and a cough," said Feorin admiringly. A second later he pouted, adding, "But it should have been mine. I could have taken you to the telephone as easily as Milka."

"I'm senior, so I get any bonuses," said Milka. "Right. Let's go."

She stalked off down the corridor, closely followed by Leaf. Leaf figured that she only had a short space of time before Milka figured out she'd been tricked.

Milka went up to the noon door and knocked. When no answer came, she opened the door and ushered Leaf in.

"Noon's office," she said. "He must be up with Lady Friday. He's got a phone on his desk."

Leaf looked around the room. It was furnished much as a modern manager's office in a hospital might be. There was no sign of a telephone.

"Where's the phone?" asked Leaf.

"Oh, it will be in the desk drawer, I expect," said Milka.

"Right," said Leaf. She dumped the pillowcases by the door, quickly crossed the room, sat down, and opened the top drawer. Her hands shook as she saw a red box, exactly like the one that Arthur had kept in his room. She swiftly took it out, opened it, and picked up the old-fashioned two-piece telephone. The earpiece crackled as she held it to her ear.

"Yes?" said a distant voice.

"I want to make a call, please," Leaf replied.

"Why else would you be talking into a telephone?" said the voice.

"Yes, I suppose," said Leaf nervously. Milka and Feorin

were waiting for her, and though they had stayed near the door, she knew they were listening. "I need to talk to Dr. Scamandros, please."

She lowered her voice and swiftly added, "He's probably in the Lower House. Or maybe the Great Maze."

"The Lower House? They're cut off, by order of Superior Saturday. Can't connect you there, nor anywhere below the Middle House."

"But it's very important," pleaded Leaf. "Please!"

"Who is this calling —" the voice started, but before it could continue, it was cut off and a new voice came in, much stronger.

"Get off, you imposter! Operator here."

"Operator? Who was that, then? Uh, never mind." Leaf's precious time was evaporating. "Please, I need to speak to Dr. Scamandros urgently. He's in . . . ah —"

"Friend of Arthur's, are you?" asked the operator.

"Yes!" said Leaf without thinking. "Or . . . no . . . depending on why you're asking."

"Putting you through. Might not last, though. Saturday's minions are all through the lines."

There was a loud click, a buzz that to Leaf's dispirited ears sounded like disconnection, then a distant voice echoed in the earpiece.

"Hello! Hello?"

"Dr. Scamandros! It's Leaf. I'm at Lady Friday's mountain retreat out in the Secondary Realms. Maybe near the Magellanic Clouds or something. I need —"

"Leaf! Keep talking so I can make a note of your exact location. Where is my locating pencil?"

Scamandros kept muttering. Leaf looked at Milka and Feorin. Milka was tilting her head, listening more intently.

"I'm meant to arrange for the shipment of fixed coughs and ailments to the Denizens here," said Leaf quickly. "Lady Friday's here, of course, and about fifty other Denizens."

"Keep talking! Does Friday have her Key?"

"I think so," said Leaf. Milka was walking over to her now. "A mirror? Now about those coughs, they probably need two each —"

"This telephone connection is forbidden," said the first voice that had come onto the line. "Action is being taken."

The telephone shook in Leaf's hands and began to emit wisps of steam. She dropped it on the desk but kept talking, putting her face as close to the fallen mouthpiece as she dared.

"Scamandros! It's the gray mold planet, I think! There's some connection from a laundry on Earth —"

The phone bubbled and hissed and melted into a blob of unsightly muck that smelled like burnt hair.

"*Hmm,*" said Milka. "So it was all a trick."

"Yes," said Leaf defiantly.

"We'd better get out of here, then," said Milka. She grabbed Leaf and turned to the door. "Feorin, pick up those pillowcases. Back to our room, quick!"

"Why?" asked Feorin. "It's not our fault.... Noon won't blame ... oh ..."

Milka was already out the door, Leaf under her arm. Feorin picked up the pillowcases and followed, forgetting to shut the door after him. Thirty seconds later, all three of them were in Milka and Feorin's room, a much smaller, shabbier, and eccentric chamber dominated by two work-tables covered in books, papers, and bookbinding tools. In one corner sat a five-foot-tall book press that had been partially taken apart, a spanner still lying on the floor next to it.

"Thanks," Leaf said as Milka set her down on the floor. "But why —"

"Shut up!" instructed Milka. "You've got us in enough trouble already. Let me think."

"Will Noon really blame us?" asked Feorin.

"Blame us!" shrieked Milka. "You're already on probation! He'll send us down to circle zero! Do you fancy fighting all the plants that get in down there?"

"What will we do?" asked Feorin anxiously.

"Hide," said Milka. "If Noon doesn't see us, he can't ask us anything."

"How long for?"

"Forever!"

"Forever?"

"For a few days anyway. Noon will forget once he gets a new phone. As for you —"

Milka advanced on Leaf angrily. The girl retreated before her, almost falling over the pile of pillowcases that Feorin had dropped on the floor.

"Can't I come hide with you?" Leaf asked.

"No!" Milka raised her fist but then let it fall without striking Leaf. "Definitely not. Get out! And don't tell anyone what you've done, or that we helped you!"

"Okay." Leaf picked up the pillowcases and backed out, Feorin obligingly holding the door open. "Thanks!"

"'Thanks'!" growled Milka. "You're more trouble than Feorin!"

The door slammed behind Leaf, leaving her alone in the corridor. But she no longer felt alone. Dr. Scamandros knew her situation, even if he didn't know her exact location. That meant Arthur would soon know, and her friend would organize a rescue as soon as possible.

All she had to do now was find Aunt Mango and

then — taking a leaf, so to speak, from Milka's book — hide with her until the rescuing forces arrived.

Leaf smiled and walked away — straight into a very tall, impeccably dressed Denizen with straw-blond hair and a very shiny monocle over one of his piercing blue eyes. Though he had not been wearing the monocle previously, Leaf instantly recognized him as being one of the two Denizens who had preceded Lady Friday's march through the hospital.

"Ah," said the Denizen, who could only be Friday's Noon. "The unauthorized use of my telephone is explained. Miss Leaf, is it not?"

Leaf nodded.

"You are fortunate that milady has ordered you to be kept in reasonable working order, as being of potential further use," drawled Noon. "That being the case, if you tell me who you called, I shall not punish you too heavily."

"I . . . I couldn't get through," said Leaf. "One of Saturday's Denizens had replaced the operator."

"Plausible," said Noon. "A most competent lie, if it is not the truth. Now, how shall we keep you out of trouble until you are required, *hmmm*?"

Leaf didn't answer. She raised her chin a half-inch and tried to look Noon in the eye, but the reflection from the monocle was too bright and she had to lid her eyes half-shut.

"One of your mortal poets said it well," said Noon. "He put milady on to the notion in the first place. 'To sleep, perchance to dream.' I think it is time you slept, Miss Leaf."

Leaf responded by throwing the pillowcases at Friday's Noon and running away. But she had gone no more than a dozen paces when she felt a fierce buffet of air and was knocked to the ground, Noon standing over her with his yellow wings at full extension across the corridor.

Leaf began to crawl away. Friday's Noon did not try to stop her. He took a small silver cone from his pocket and raised it to his lips, to use as a megaphone.

"Sleep, Miss Leaf." Noon's voice had transformed itself into Lady Friday's, stronger than it had ever sounded before. Leaf was tired, so tired from everything she had been through; she had done everything she could. . . .

Leaf stopped crawling and lay still. Friday's Noon replaced the silver cone within his coat and spoke to unseen Denizens behind him.

"Take her to the bed turner. Tell him she is to be carefully tended. Milady may have need of her, in time to come."

Chapter Sixteen

There were nine Artful Loungers who swooped with darkened wings upon the raft, each bearing a curved sword of blue steel in his or her right hand and a long crystal stiletto in the left. The stilettos could only be used once, as they contained a core of Nothing that would kill even a Denizen. Dangerous weapons, they lasted only a few hours from their manufacture, for the Nothing would soon eat its way out of its sorcerous confinement in the crystal.

The leading Lounger never even made it to the deck, Ugham's powerfully thrown spear arresting his flight with a vengeance. But the other eight landed in formation and advanced upon Cool of the Evening, Arthur, Suzy, Fred, and Ugham. Of Pirkin and the other Paper Pushers there was no sign, though all had been on deck only moments before, with Pirkin close to Arthur.

"Leave at once!" commanded Arthur, raising the Key. But he did not call upon its power, and the Artful Loungers did not respond. They smiled their vacant smiles and kept coming, their glossy patent leather shoes and checked trousers all in step, their pastel-blue peasant smocks all unbuttoned in exactly the same careful, careless way, their berets all at the same angle.

"Ready," muttered Ugham. As he spoke, the Loungers rushed forward and everything became a mad blur of movement, of trying to hit Loungers while not being hit, particularly by the Nothing-core stilettos. Arthur almost felt as if his body was reacting without his conscious direction, so swiftly did everything happen, muscles acting purely from training, reflex, and fear.

Then it was over, as quickly as it had begun. Arthur stood amid four dead Loungers, surprise still on their faces that they had been so easily slain by mere sword-wounds, not knowing they had been hit by the Fourth Key. The other four were backing away, and they kept on retreating until they were far enough away to turn and fling themselves up into the night.

Arthur looked down at himself and saw he was not harmed, not even marked by a scratch. He quickly turned to check the others. They were several feet behind him and he realized that he must have charged forward as the Loungers attacked.

"Anyone hurt?" he asked as he walked back to them. Though there was no spoken agreement, everyone then moved back several paces farther still, to put more space between themselves and the dead Artful Loungers. Arthur kept his back to them. He did not want to see his handi-work. "Those knives looked bad."

"Poison blades," said Ugham. "But I have taken no scathe. You bore the brunt of it, Lord Arthur."

"I never even got close to one," said Fred.

"Me neither," said Suzy with a shudder. "And that's the way I like it."

"Cool of the Evening?" asked Arthur. The Winged Servant of the Night was still standing on one leg. "No new wounds?"

She signed a message to Fred.

"She says not," he translated. "Uh, she wants to know who you are, Arthur. I guess smelling right isn't every-thing."

"I am Arthur, the Rightful Heir to the Architect."

"Master of the Lower House, Lord of the Far Reaches," added Suzy.

"Duke of the Border Sea and Commander-in-Chief of the Army of the Architect," added Fred.

Arthur grimaced. It still felt weird to hear all that.

Cool of the Evening bowed her head slightly, but did not sign a message.

"And that is Suzy Turquoise Blue, Monday's Tierce,"

said Arthur. "And Lieutenant Fred Initial Numbers Gold and Banneret Ugham of the Piper's Newniths. We are in temporary alliance with Banneret Ugham."

Fred made a squeaking sound and put his hand up.

"Arthur? Do you mean it? Me, Lieutenant Gold?"

"Yes," said Arthur. "I'd make you a General, but I figure you might find it easier to start off being an officer a bit lower down."

"You can make me a General if you like, Arthur," said Suzy. "I mean, Monday's Tierce is all very well, but when it comes to rotten jobs being dished out, I reckon a General gets to have less of them —"

"I'll think about it," said Arthur. "I'm not sure you'd be a very responsible General, Suzy. Anyway, the most important thing is that we're all friends. At least I hope —"

Cool of the Evening looked up and made a rapid sign.

"What? More Loungers?" asked Arthur. He raised his rapier, eyes scanning the sky.

"Nope," said Fred. "More Winged Servants of the Night. Uh, I hope they know we're on their side."

Arthur hastily lowered his rapier. Ugham, who had been retrieving his spear, grounded that weapon. Suzy tucked her knife back into her belt. The Paper Pushers were still not in evidence, and for the first time Arthur wondered where they could have gone.

That thought went away as twenty or more Winged Servants of the Night descended, only becoming visible as they entered the band of sunlight, which the raft had almost left. It had been moving swiftly up the canal the whole time, and Arthur had grown used to both the tilted "deck" beneath his feet and the faint sunshine. But soon they would be in darkness once more, though the raft would continue its upward passage for many more hours.

"Tell them we're friends, please," said Arthur to Cool of the Evening. She nodded and raised her arms to send a more visible, semaphore-style message with her arms.

"What did she say?" whispered Suzy to Fred.

He shook his head and whispered back, "Haven't a clue. I know they have big signs and little signs. Big signs are with arms only, and I never learned them."

Most of the Winged Servants circled above the raft, moving with it, but three came down to land. Cool of the Evening hopped to meet them, and there was a very fast conversation in sign language that went on for several minutes.

"Too quick for me," said Fred. "I can only get a few words. She's telling them who you are, Arthur."

"That could be trouble." Arthur kept looking up at the Servants overhead, watching in case they suddenly dove. "If they're fighting because they're loyal to Friday, then they'll have to attack. Keep ready. Where are those Paper Pushers? Pirkin was right next to me. . . ."

"I'm here," said a muffled voice several yards away. It sounded like it was coming from the region of Arthur's feet.

Arthur looked down. He couldn't see anything but the usual bundles of papyrus records for a moment, then he caught sight of Pirkin peering out through a narrow gap.

"How . . . how did you get in there?" asked Arthur. The gap between the bundles was only as wide as his hand.

"You can push the bundles apart," said Pirkin. "If you know how. Then there are lots of gaps and airspaces through the structure. 'Course, only members of the Association are allowed to manipulate the structure of —"

"Right!" said Arthur. He was relieved to find that Pirkin hadn't somehow been killed or fallen off the raft.

"And I'm staying here!" said Pirkin. "Till we need to change currents anyway. Which should be in about —"

"Here they come," said Fred.

Arthur swiftly looked back up, but the Servants above were still circling. The three who had been with Cool of the Evening were advancing, their hands held wide and open, to show they held no weapons — at least none more dangerous than the claws on their gloves. Cool of the Evening herself sat down where she was.

"Hello," said Arthur as the Servants stopped a few paces away and made short bows. "Um, Fred here can do some of your signs. . . ."

All three of the newly arrived Servants immediately signed to Fred.

"Uh, this is . . . let's see . . . Turned Wingfeather Flys Surprisingly Well, Ferocious Slayer of the Pre-Dawn, and One Who Survived the Darkness. Ah, One Who Survived the Darkness is the highest-ranking in House precedence; she reports directly to Friday's Dusk."

One Who Survived the Darkness was the middle Servant and was fractionally taller than the other two. The claws of her gloves were also a pallid white, Arthur noticed, like carved moonstones, unlike the others, who had claws of some dark, metallic substance.

"She says thanks for helping Cool of the Evening," said Fred.

"No problem," said Arthur. "Any enemy of Superior Saturday's is a friend of ours."

" 'The Winged Servants of the Night carry out our duty,' " translated Fred. " 'To patrol the night of the Middle House and slaughter Nithlings and . . . um, I think . . . unauthorized travelers, to rend them with our claws and burn them with the fire of our weapons.' "

"Tell them we're authorized, Arthur," said Suzy.

One Who Survived the Darkness turned her masked face to Suzy and made a series of rapid signs.

"Uh-oh," said Fred. "You are not authorized. Oh, it's all right. She says, 'Usually we would either kill you or take you to Dusk for judgment. But Dusk has gone, and Lady Friday too. Dawn, who claims to speak for them, is not our master. You are Lord Arthur, and master of much of the House, so a distinguished visitor. Better, you have fought for us. We will not harm you or your minions —'"

"Hang on," muttered Suzy. "Who are you calling —"

"Suzy!" warned Arthur. "Let Fred finish."

" 'We owe you a debt, and will help you if we can.' "

Arthur directed a quelling glare at Suzy, who was about to open her mouth again, and then bowed to One Who Survived the Darkness. That gave him a moment to think.

"Thank you," he said slowly. "I think you can help us . . . help me . . . if you are able to carry myself and my companions up to the Top Shelf. I need to find a sorcerer there, and quickly."

One Who Survived the Darkness tilted her masked head to the side quizzically, then signed to Fred.

"She says they can fly us up there. But the High Guild are not to be trusted. Also, Friday's Dawn and his Gilded

Youths are encamped outside Binding Junction and she doesn't know what they plan or where their allegiance lies."

"We'll just have to chance it," said Arthur. "It's going to take too long to get there by raft."

"Four of them can carry one of us," translated Fred after a flurry of signs. "How many are to go?"

"The three of us," said Arthur, glancing at Ugham. "I'm sorry, Ugham, but there's a chance the Piper will be ahead of us —"

"My task is to escort Miss Suzy and Lieutenant Fred," rumbled Ugham. "To do so, I must stand at their side."

"But if we meet the Piper and he orders you to attack us —" said Arthur.

"What can even a warrior such as I do against the mighty Arthur and his sword?" asked Ugham. "I think you have little to fear, Lord Arthur."

"Let him come," said Suzy. "He's just a turnip farmer underneath."

"It does not become you to make jest of my ambition, Miss Suzy," said Ugham.

Arthur looked at Fred questioningly.

"I reckon he's more help than hindrance," said Fred. "And now that Suzy and I don't have to obey, the odds are better."

"You'd still answer to the Piper's pipe," said Arthur. He bit his lower lip, unconsciously flicking it under his front teeth several times. "Oh, all right. Ugham can come too. Four of us, then."

One Who Survived the Darkness nodded and made arm signals to the Servants above, who immediately began to descend. The first two landed next to Cool of the Evening, and one of them took out a pair of wings that might have suited a doll, being no more than six inches long. But as the Servant shook them, they grew, and a few seconds later both Servants were helping Cool of the Evening detach her old wings and put on new ones.

"Hey," said Suzy. "If they've got wings, they can just give *us* some. Beats being carried."

One Who Survived the Darkness made an emphatic sign.

"Ah, that's 'No'!" said Fred. "Guess they haven't got enough."

"Or they don't want us flying around," said Arthur. "Never mind. As long as we get up to the Top Shelf faster than on this raft."

"It was good enough for you before!" protested a voice from below. The Servants jumped at the sound of it, wings flapping and hands going to weapons.

"First it's 'Give us a ride even if it's against the rules,' " Pirkin continued. "Now, it's 'Your raft's too slow.' There'll be a minute of protest issued by the next meeting of the Association, I can tell you!"

"We're very grateful, Pirkin," said Arthur. "For the clothes, the hot water, the ride on the raft. Everything. I shall personally see to it that you and your crew are commended if . . . when . . . I take over the Middle House."

"Those clothes are property of the Assoc —" Pirkin started to say. "Commended? What, with a certificate and all?"

"A big framed certificate," Arthur promised. "With all my seals on it, for all the demesnes from the Lower House on up."

"Well, that's handsome," said Pirkin. "And if the Noble and Exalted Association of Waterway Motivators can ever be of help to you, you know where to find us. On the canal!"

Pirkin's skinny arm reached up out of the gap in the reeds. Arthur shook the Denizen's hand, then it was withdrawn and a moment later the gap closed. Pirkin, however pleased he was with a potential commendation, was not going to risk coming out.

"We need to go, Arthur," said Fred. "The Servants hold the skylock above but there is the risk of a counterattack. And they need to be back in their eyrie before dawn."

"Where is that?" asked Arthur.

All three Servants hissed and made the "no" sign, then One Who Survived the Darkness made a few more. The three launched themselves into the air and other Servants joined them to flutter a dozen feet above the heads of Arthur and his friends.

"It's a secret," said Fred. "Up anyway. Oh, they want us to lie on our stomachs and hold up our legs and arms. Easier for them to pick us up that way."

"Or kill us," muttered Suzy, very quietly. "Not that I s'pose they're going to."

"I think we can trust them," Arthur whispered back. He put away the Fourth Key and checked to make sure it was securely on his belt, and that the crystal with the speck of the Architect's gold leaf was secure in an inside pocket. "They could have attacked us straight away. And Fred wanted to be one, so they can't be all bad."

"I wanted to be a Nithling with three heads once, so that's no guarantee," whispered Suzy as she lay down and raised her arms and feet. "What's more, after a washing between the ears I thought it was possible."

Arthur smiled but the smile only lasted a moment as he caught sight of the four dead Artful Loungers. Though they were Denizens and stranger-than-usual ones at that, and enemies, he still felt bad that they were dead, at his hand.

All this fighting is so unnecessary, he thought as he lay down and put up his hands and feet. *I guess the sooner I have the Fifth Key, the better, so I can try to stop it. Not that I've managed to completely stop the fighting with the Piper's Newniths in the Great Maze. I just wish the Trustees would give up and hand over the Keys, like they were supposed to do in the first place. Then I could . . .*

Arthur's thoughts were distracted as he felt the rush of air from four sets of Servant wings. Four pairs of Servants' hands carefully grabbed his wrists and ankles, their claws withdrawn. Then, with an even greater downdraft from the beating wings, he was airborne.

Arthur did not want to pick up his train of thought, at least in part because he was uncomfortable about where it was going. But he couldn't help but linger on it for a moment longer.

What am I going to do if I somehow do manage to defeat the last three Morrow Days and get all the Keys? If I can just get home . . . keep the family safe . . . stay human . . .

Chapter Seventeen

"My arms and legs are going to come out and my body is going to drop like a horrible lump if we don't land soon!" shouted Suzy.

"It can't be too long," Arthur shouted back, though he actually had no idea how long it would be. His shoulders and hips hurt terribly too, but there wasn't much point in complaining about it.

They'd passed the first skylock fairly quickly after leaving the raft, witnessing a brief skirmish between twenty or thirty winged Artful Loungers and an unclear number of Winged Servants, who they only saw in the flashes of firewash from their projectors or when they tussled hand to hand with the more illuminated enemy.

It was much warmer in the Middle of the Middle, which was a relief to Arthur. Being frozen as well as having your arms and legs pulled out by the joints had nothing to recommend it.

Not that they stayed in the Middle of the Middle for long. The Servants had kept climbing at a steady rate and they had gone through the second skylock an hour after the first. This passage was not marked by any combat, and indeed Arthur might not even have known they'd gone through it if it hadn't been for Suzy calling out that she could see the hole in the sky.

The Top Shelf was warmer still, almost tropical. Arthur would have found it unpleasant, save that he had been so cold before, he welcomed any heat. But given that it was still night, he figured it must get very warm during its day, depending on what kind of sun or suns it had.

"I hope it's soon," shouted Suzy. "Can you see anything below?"

Since passing through the second skylock, the Servants had leveled off, lending hope that their destination was close.

"I espy campfires below," called out Ugham. Arthur couldn't see the Newnith or the Servants who carried him, but he sounded quite close. Craning his neck, Arthur looked around to see if he could pick up the campfires too, though all he'd previously spotted were a few stars high above. He'd watched them for a while to see if they moved, but they hadn't.

"I see them!" shouted Fred. "Guess that's Friday's Dawn and the Gilded Youths."

Arthur turned to where he thought Fred was flying and caught sight of a whole bunch of tiny twinkling orange-red lights below them and a mile or more ahead.

"What do they need campfires for?" shouted Arthur. "It's hot up here and they don't need to eat!"

"Tradition!" yelled Suzy. "Or tea, maybe. What's a camp without a fire anyhow? Oh, I see other lights."

Arthur squinted ahead. There were pallid white dots beyond and above the crescent-shape of the campfires.

"That must be Binding Junction," called out Fred. "The High Guild's headquarters."

A minute later the Servants began to glide down, affirming Fred's guess. They swooped low enough above the camp to see the actual fires, passing only fifty feet or so above the many Denizens who were sitting or standing around them. Strangely, no alarm was raised or even any notice given to the outsiders' appearance.

Perhaps they just don't look up, thought Arthur. *I guess they know the Winged Servants control the sky at night. . . .*

Binding Junction lay ahead, a dim silhouette. As far as Arthur could tell, it was a fortress with four corner towers and one large central tower, or keep. The Servants were heading for this, and indeed almost before Arthur could prepare himself, he and his friends were being dropped on the battlements of this huge, square tower.

"Thanks," grunted Arthur as he tried to stand upright. Every muscle and joint in his arms and legs ached, and it was very hard to straighten out.

The Servants bowed, and one of them — who might or might not have been One Who Survived the Darkness — rapidly signed at Fred. Then all of them were gone, off into the night, which Arthur now noted was tinged to the east with the first faint colorful hints of a rising sun.

"They're in a hurry," said Fred. "Daylight's coming."

Arthur nodded and stretched again, biting back a shriek of pain. Suzy had no such compunction and let out a series of yells as she massaged her own shoulders.

Arthur stopped stretching and looked around to see if the noise had attracted any unwanted attention. The battlements were deserted as far as he could see. There was an open staircase in one corner, pale lamplight spreading from its entrance. Ugham was already there, looking down the steps.

"Guess we'd better go find a representative of the High Guild of . . . what was it . . . Binding and something else?" Arthur suggested.

"Restoration," said Fred. "Remember, they've got a reputation for being tricky."

"I only need them to supply a sorcerer to do one spell," said Arthur. "We won't be staying long."

"What do you want the sorcerer to do?" Suzy asked as they started down the steps, Ugham leading the way with Arthur close behind. There were candles — or candle equivalents, since they looked the part but just glowed without a visible flame — stuck in iron sconces every few yards. There was also a shabby carpet tacked on the stone steps, which made the descent slippery and forced Arthur to concentrate for a few steps before he could answer.

"I want them to turn the speck of the Architect's gold foil into a kind of compass," he finally said. "To point to other bits of the same gold foil, which were used in the Will. Apparently something separated from a larger whole is still sorcerously part of the bigger lot. Scamandros told me about it."

"So it will lead us to the Will?" asked Fred.

"I hope so."

"But you could have done that with the Key," said Suzy. "You don't need a —"

She stopped talking suddenly. Arthur didn't need to turn around to know that Fred had elbowed her in the stomach.

"If they can't do it here, I will use the Key," said Arthur quietly. "But not until then."

"Someone comes!" warned Ugham. He pressed himself back against the wall and leveled his spear, just as a

Denizen hurried around the curve of the stair, almost spitting himself.

"Oh!" exclaimed the Denizen, stepping quickly back down. He was over six feet tall and handsome, save for an oddly short nose and flat face, so he was probably quite important. This impression was aided by his black velvet robes, which were embroidered with a complex scene showing Denizens working a huge book press, ten times their own height. The embroidery was so fine it looked almost like an illustration printed on the fabric. He also wore a stiff paper hat like a bishop's miter, though more triangular, its two longest edges marked like a ruler, with five divisions marked by strange numerals.

"Ugham," said Arthur, with a gesture. The Newnith shortened his grip on his spear, bringing it back to his side, at the ready.

"I do beg your pardon," said the Denizen. He bowed twice and wrung his ink-stained hands together. "Am I correct in assuming that I address Lord Arthur, Rightful Heir to the Architect?"

"Yes, I'm Arthur."

"The High Guild welcomes you to Binding Junction, Lord Arthur." The Denizen performed yet another (and even lower) bow, so low even his flattened nose almost scraped the steps above where he stood. "I am Master Binder Jakem, First Pressmaster, 1,000th in precedence within the House and, with the absence of Lady Friday's Noon, in authority over the High Guild of Binding and Restoration. I apologize for not being ready to receive you when you alighted above, but we only just received word of your arrival —"

"Who from?" asked Suzy.

Jakem ignored her and continued. "But in any case, we naturally wish to do whatever we can to make your visit enjoyable. Perhaps you might like to take a tour of the presses? Or begin with a cup of tea in our . . . though I say it myself . . . charming executive tearoom?"

"A cup of tea would be good," said Arthur. "But I haven't got time to waste, so if along with a cup of tea you can provide your best sorcerer, that would be better still."

"A cup and sorcerer, ha-ha!" replied Jakem.

Nobody laughed, and the Denizen's hand-wringing increased.

"Just my little joke. Naturally, I am the most accomplished of us in sorcerous arts, though I must confess in a somewhat narrow field related to our work. But please, follow me to the executive tearoom, and pray do tell me what it is that you require, Lord Arthur."

Arthur explained what he wanted as Jakem led the

way, out of the tower stair and along a stone-walled corridor that was hung with tapestries depicting Denizens sewing, gluing, and pressing books, as well as chiseling tablets of stone and casting type from molten metal, presumably lead.

"That shouldn't be a problem, Lord Arthur," said Jakem. "Linking objects that were once together is a simple matter of rebinding and falls within our purview."

He opened a door and led the way down another corridor, this one draped in white sheets like a painter's drop covers. This white-wrapped passage led to a chamber whose walls were also draped with sheets, some of them splashed with paint. Apart from the drop cloths, the room looked very comfortable, with half a dozen armchairs richly upholstered in a plum-colored material adorned with pictograms in gold thread. Numerous cushions that together traversed the full spectrum of a rainbow were piled on the chairs, and in the middle there was a table carved from a single block of gold-flecked stone with a silver tray and tea service on it.

"The renovations are not yet complete!" said Jakem crossly. "I do apologize, Lord Arthur. Would you care to take tea in the Lower Common Room instead?"

"Here will do," said Arthur. "Provided you fix up that spell on the gold leaf right away."

"Of course, of course," said Jakem. "Please, do sit down. Shall I pour?"

Arthur and the others sat down, save for Ugham, who stood between Suzy's and Fred's chairs. Jakem snapped his fingers and the teapot jumped and let forth a burst of steam. He then poured cups for everyone, handed the small cups delicately balanced on saucers around, took one himself, and sat down on the chair nearest the corridor entrance.

"This is a special blend, imported from the Secondary Realms, not made in the Lower Reaches." Jakem sniffed at the steam from his cup. "Ahh! Delightful. But I understand your impatience, Lord Arthur."

He set the cup and saucer down on the arm of his chair and stood.

"I shall just fetch the few tools I need," he said, quickly stepping back into the corridor. As he reached it, he shouted three words in an unknown language, words that Arthur felt vibrate in his chest. Words of sorcery and power.

With that shout, the white sheets whipped back to reveal open space, the real walls some twenty or thirty feet away. The ceiling above was also revealed as a huge slab of green-painted bronze, because it was the top plate of an enormous book press, with Arthur and his friends sitting right in the middle, on top of the bottom plate.

"Caught!" shouted Jakem, wringing his hands again, this time in glee.

"What are you going on about?" asked Arthur wearily. "We'll just walk out."

The press wasn't moving, and though he couldn't see directly above the plate, he could see one of the arms of the press about thirty feet up, with ten Denizens there standing ready to push the arm, walking around a circular gallery like an internal verandah. He knew there would be a giant screw above the plate and that by pushing the arms clockwise or counterclockwise the Denizens could open or close the press. But it wouldn't be a quick process.

"Not from the Architect's own press, made for the binding of very difficult things!" crowed Jakem. "And not when you're drugged by *ghowchem* tea, for good measure!"

Arthur frowned and his hand fell to the Key at his side.

"The Key won't help you either." Jakem laughed. "Not if we press you very slowly, so it does not react to a sharp threat! We have had particular advice on that!"

Arthur frowned again. His arm did feel strangely heavy, and it was true that the Key was quiescent, not leaping into his hand or turning into its rapier form.

"Start the press down!" ordered Jakem. "Half-speed!"

Chapter Eighteen

"I had heard the High Guild was treacherous," said Arthur. He sat up straighter in his chair, which took considerable effort. It felt like he had a sack of cement tied to his chest and back.

"We are merely pragmatic," said Jakem.

"And knowing that," said Arthur, "I didn't drink the tea."

With a gasp, he stood up. The gasp was echoed by Jakem.

"I bet my friends didn't either," added Arthur. He wasted no effort by looking around as he said that, and he heard no answer. But even if they hadn't drunk the tea, the others would probably be held silent and in place by the powers of the press.

"You can't get up!" protested Jakem. "The press was made by the Architect! It has never failed to hold recalcitrants!"

"This was made by the Architect too," said Arthur. He took a step and drew the Key, willing it to take its sword form. For a moment he thought it wouldn't work, then the baton slowly lengthened and shimmered, transforming into a thin silver blade, the graceful quillons of the hilt wrapped around Arthur's fist.

"Stop the press," ordered Arthur. He took another step, directly towards Jakem. It hurt to walk, with every muscle in his legs, back, and arms feeling like they were being twisted by the fingers of a sadistic masseur. But he had kept going before, when he had no air to breathe, when only his determination kept him moving. This was only pain, not lack of breath.

"But you *can't*!" protested Jakem. "You simply *can't* be walking out!"

Arthur did not reply. He took another step and snarled with the effort. His arms and legs were shaking, but he forced himself on. Only four more steps and he would be clear of the base plate — and within striking distance of Jakem, if the Denizen didn't flee.

"Perhaps we have been a little overhasty," said Jakem. Three more steps.

"We were ordered to, you see," said Jakem. "We have to follow orders."

Arthur gritted his teeth together. It was only two more steps but he couldn't lift his foot, it was just too hard.

Instead, he slid his right foot forward and let out a sound that to him sounded like a moan of pain, but to Jakem sounded like a growl of anger.

"Stop the press!" shouted Jakem. "Lord Arthur, we most humbly apologize!"

Arthur slid his left foot off the base plate of the press. Immediately the weight fell off him, so suddenly that he bounded forward and the point of his rapier accidentally flew to Jakem's face. Arthur only just managed to twitch his wrist so the blade cleared the Denizen's forehead by two inches and drilled a hole straight through his paper hat.

Jakem fell to the ground as Arthur recovered, bringing the rapier back to the guard position with the Denizen's hat halfway along the blade. As he slid the hat off, Arthur looked over his shoulder. Suzy was hurrying to his side, her knife in her hand. Ugham had leaped clear of the press and was looking up at the Denizens in the winding gallery, his spear ready. Only Fred was still in his chair, sitting immobile, with his eyes open.

Maybe he's dead, thought Arthur, struck by this sudden fear. *He'd be trusting enough to drink. . . .*

"Get up!" ordered Arthur. He tapped Jakem on the head with his rapier. "Get someone to give Fred an antidote for whatever you put in the tea."

Jakem rose unsteadily, his hands clasped in supplication.

"There is no antidote —"

Arthur snarled and pulled his hand back, ready to stab with the rapier.

"But it is merely a soporific!" said Jakem. "A little sleep-maker, that's all. Your friend will wake within the hour!"

"Too trusting, that lad," said Suzy. "Should've learned to never drink a tea you can see through."

"What?" asked Arthur. His hand was shaking — not, he thought, from the effort of crossing the floor of the press, but from repressing the surge of anger he'd felt towards Jakem. He'd really wanted to kill the Denizen for a second, and if Fred had been killed or even harmed, he thought he would have.

"Tea," said Suzy. "Got to be thick and dark, or it's no good."

Arthur shook his head. He was tired again, he realized. He'd had a good sleep after the siege of the Citadel but that was at least twenty hours ago.

No time to sleep, he thought, with a glance at Fred. Ugham had moved to look at the boy and now he nodded and gestured with his hand, indicating the rise and fall of a chest, to show the boy was breathing.

Sleep can come after . . . after what? Don't think about that . . . think about what has to be done. . . .

"Right," he said. "Jakem, get two of your Denizens to move Fred and his chair out of the press. They can put him over there. Were you telling the truth about the spell on the gold leaf?"

"Yes, Lord Arthur!" said Jakem. "Digby, Hurrent, fetch Mister Fred out of the press. Quickly now, you dolts!"

"Do you need anything to do the spell?" asked Arthur.

"No, it is a simple matter," said Jakem. "If I may hold the gold leaf?"

Arthur reached inside his coat and got out the crystal prism with the speck of gold leaf inside.

"Just do the spell I want," he warned as he handed it over. "I want to be able to use it to find Part Five of the Will."

"Yes, sir, I understand," said Jakem. "It should work as you wish, the gold leaf here calling out to the greater part that was used in the creation of the Will."

"I don't want it pointing to Dame Primus, though," added Arthur. "That's the current shape of Parts One to Four of the Will."

"It will point to whichever part of the Will is closest," said Jakem. "Providing, of course, that this speck of gold is in fact part of the greater whole the Architect used."

"He talks a lot, doesn't he?" said Suzy. "You should stick him a bit, Arthur, for encouragement."

"Not with the Key," said Arthur. "It only needs a touch to kill."

"Please, Lord Arthur!" groveled Jakem. "If I may concentrate for a moment?"

Arthur nodded and looked at Suzy, who correctly interpreted his look as a sign to keep silent. She shrugged, smiled, and wandered over to Fred, who had just been carried out of the press.

Jakem drew out a large piece of stiff paper from one of the pockets of his robe and put it down on the floor with the crystal sitting in the middle. Then he took a quill pen and tiny bottle of activated ink from another pocket and, crouching down on his knees, quickly inked the pen and swiftly wrote four incomprehensible words from an alien alphabet on the paper around the crystal. The words were hardly written when they began to float up off the paper, shimmering and writhing like strange sea creatures on the tide. Jakem waved the quill above them in a ritual fashion and the words slid into the crystal, shrinking as they entered, till they were too small to see.

The Pressmaster sniffed, put the lid back on the ink, replaced pen and bottle in a pocket, and stood up.

"There, it's done," he said.

"That's it?" said Arthur. "Okay, you pick it up."

"I would not dare essay anything against you, milord —" Jakem said.

"Pick it up, then," interrupted Arthur. "And hand it to one of your Denizens. He can give it to me."

"Better give it to me, Arthur," said Suzy suspiciously. "Then you can stick 'im if there's anything havey-cavey going on with it."

"I have done the spell exactly as instructed!" bleated Jakem. He bent down and picked up the crystal. "Digby! Come here!"

The denizen Digby ran over, pausing to tug his forelock in front of Arthur before accepting the crystal from Jakem. Nothing odd occurred then, or when it was passed to Suzy. She held it up to look carefully at the speck of gold inside, knocked on it with the handle of her knife, and finally handed it to Arthur, who took it with his left hand, not wanting to let go of the Key. Jakem was just too smooth. He oozed potential for treachery.

"Looks all right, but I'm ready," Suzy said, sidling over to Jakem with her knife out. He looked at her nervously and began to wring his hands again.

Arthur gazed into the crystal.

"How do I make it work?" he asked, but even as he

spoke, he saw that the speck itself was moving within the crystal and changing shape. Slowly it became a very thin and very small arrow, the size of a fingernail clipping. It spun around a little and then settled down to point in a particular direction, at a vertical angle.

"That way," he said, pointing at a spot near where Fred was sleeping in his chair. "And up, I think. What lies that way and up, Jakem?"

"The mountain," said Jakem. "Lady Friday's Scriptorium."

"How long till morning?" asked Arthur.

"Dawn breaks even now," Jakem said. "The little sun is already up, the greater one in a few minutes."

"We'll need wings," said Arthur. "Or is there some other way to get to the Scriptorium?"

Jakem shook his head.

"What does that mean?" snapped Arthur. "No other way or no wings?"

"No other way," said Jakem, flinching. "It may only be reached through flight. As for wings, we have none, but perhaps Friday's Dawn . . . the Gilded Youths . . ."

"Who you haven't let in," said Arthur. "Why was that?"

"Saturday's Noon instructed us, I think because Friday's Dawn refused to obey. We were only following Saturday's orders!"

"Is Saturday's Noon still here?" asked Arthur. "Are your elevators working? And your telephones?"

"No, Saturday's Noon visited only briefly yesterday. Saturday's Dusk has visited several times through the night, but he is not here now. The elevators answer to them, but not to us. Our telephones are not working."

"I want you to send a messenger to Friday's Dawn," instructed Arthur. "Tell him that Lord Arthur has assumed command of the Middle House and if he will follow my orders, he will be put in charge of this fortress and the Top Shelf."

"This fortress!" squeaked Jakem. "But Dawn's province is the Flat, down there —"

Arthur lifted the point of his rapier.

"Yes, at once, Lord Arthur. Digby, you dunce! You heard Lord Arthur. Get yourself an olive branch and deliver his message immediately to Friday's Dawn outside the gates."

"Get those chairs out from the press and set them up here," said Arthur. He really needed to sit down.

"Gaborl, Pluik!" shouted Jakem. "Move these chairs instantly for Lord Arthur!"

"You help them," said Suzy to Jakem. "Those chairs look heavy."

"Yes, do," said Arthur. "Don't bother with the tea, though."

Without being told to, the Denizens set up one chair by itself and the others facing it in a semicircle. Arthur settled down in the single chair. He kept the Key in its rapier form, resting the blade across the arm of the chair, holding the hilt loosely in his hand.

"Sit down," he said to Jakem, who chose a seat facing him. Suzy sat down too, while Ugham stood between her and Fred.

"Since we're going to have to wait for a response from Friday's Dawn and for Fred to wake up, you can answer some more questions," Arthur said to Jakem.

"Anything, anything, milord."

"Has the Piper been here?" Arthur couldn't help but glance at Ugham, who met his eyes with an untroubled gaze. Arthur repressed a sigh. He liked Ugham, and he liked the sound of the Newniths. As the Piper had told him before the assault on the Citadel, they actually wanted to be farmers. But even so, Ugham was a problematic ally. One word from the Piper and he would have to turn on his friends.

"Not here," answered Jakem.

Arthur didn't suppress his sigh this time.

"You mean not in Binding Junction or not in the Middle House?"

"Ah, I meant to say, he has been seen. He and a troop of his children appeared several hours ago and flew off, presumably to Friday's Scriptorium, if the Winged Servants did not intercept them first."

"Did anybody else go after him?"

"Hmm, I believe Saturday's Dusk and a dozen or so Internal Auditors might have flown after him. . . ."

"Internal Auditors?" asked Arthur.

"The most doughty soldiery of the Upper House," said Ugham. "Fell warriors, by all accounts."

"They can suck your innards out by looking at you," said Suzy. " 'Least that's what they say."

"I wonder which children the Piper had with him," said Arthur. "He must have used the Improbable Stair, or he'd have brought Newniths. That reminds me. We encountered a Nithling in the Flat, Jakem. A kind of pig thing with a horn. . . ."

"A pig thing with a horn? Ah, I do believe there was some nasty squealing coming out of the elevator Saturday's Dusk was using. . . . It could perhaps have been the type of created Nithling called a *grannow-hoinch*. . . ."

"I thought it must have come with Saturday's Dusk,"

said Arthur. "Strange combination, though. I wonder what the Fetchers were looking for. . . . Do you know, Jakem?"

"I beg your pardon, Lord Arthur?" Jakem wiped his brow nervously and went back to wringing his hands. "Do I know . . ."

"Do you know what Saturday's Fetchers were looking for down on the Flat?"

"Um, not exactly. I do believe there was some talk about something, perhaps a modified rodent, that had taken something not exactly its property. . . ."

"A Raised Rat!" exclaimed Arthur. "They were looking for a Raised Rat. I wonder what it could have taken?"

"I don't know precisely," said Jakem. "But I did happen to hear a little of the conversation between Saturday's Noon and Dusk, and that fragment leads me to think the rat — if it was a rat — might have laid its paws upon a letter."

I wonder what that's all about, thought Arthur. He rubbed his eyes in an effort to banish his weariness. *A Raised Rat who stole something, presumably from Saturday, and they're looking for it on the Flat of the Middle House. . . .*

"Reckon it must have jumped a Transfer Plate, the one Friday's messenger gave to Saturday, same as we did for the Piper's," said Suzy. "I thought I saw some funny prints in the snow when we arrived, didn't I, Uggie?"

Ugham nodded.

Arthur looked at him sharply, but this time the Newnith did not meet his gaze, instead looking into a space above Arthur's shoulder.

You know something about this, thought Arthur. *I wonder if you saw the Raised Rat. I'd better ask Fred what he saw. I hope he wakes up soon. In the meantime, maybe I could take a little rest too . . . try to think. . . .*

"I'm going to shut my eyes for a few minutes," said Arthur. "Suzy, Ugham, can you keep watch?"

"Sure," said Suzy. Ugham nodded again.

"Jakem, you're not to go anywhere or do anything, or give any orders."

"I completely understand, milord!"

Arthur looked around the room, at the press, and at the Denizens who still stood up on the winding gallery. It all looked safe enough, for the moment.

"Wake me when Digby comes back with the reply from Friday's Dawn," said Arthur, and he shut his eyes.

Chapter Nineteen

The Newnith soldier thrust with his spear, and this time it got under Arthur's shield. He saw it slide under in horrifyingly slow motion and then it hit his armor, and for a second he thought it would be all right, but it slid under that too and was about to slide into his actual stomach. The Newnith was shouting, "Friday's Dawn . . . Friday's Dawn . . . Friday's Dawn . . ."

Arthur came awake with a cry and a jump that almost tumbled him out of the chair. He felt terrible, stiff and sore all over. His joints hurt from the flight up from the canal, and his muscles hurt from escaping the press. Suzy was standing next to him, plucking his sleeve.

"Friday's Dawn is coming in! He's accepted your offer!"

Arthur blinked, wiped his eyes, and sat up straight.

"Is Fred —"

Fred waved at him from the chair opposite and gave a rueful smile.

"Sorry I drank the tea, Arthur. It was stupid of me —"

"Don't worry," said Arthur. "I almost drank it too. Uh, how long have I been asleep?"

"Around an hour," said Suzy. "That right, Jakey?"

Jakem reached into his robes and pulled out a pocket watch, flicking open the case with his thumb. He studied it intently for a few seconds, then replaced it.

"Fifty-three minutes, milord," he said. "Friday's Dawn is waiting. Do you still wish to speak to him?"

"Send him in," said Arthur.

Friday's Dawn was, as Arthur expected, a tall and handsome Denizen. But he had not expected to see one in golden plate armor that extended from ankle to neck, including a cuirass shaped with more muscles than even a Denizen could have. Long daisy-yellow wings were folded at his back, pinions rising above his head and tail feathers reaching almost to his armored ankles. He carried his visored and plumed helmet in the crook of his left arm, above a curved sword on his hip, which was balanced by some kind of short bow in a leather case on his right. A bandage around his forehead was stained with blue blood, indicating a recent wound and harsh fighting, presumably with Saturday's forces.

Dawn bowed stiffly before Arthur, who stood and inclined his head in return.

"Greetings, Lord Arthur." Dawn's voice was gravelly, not at all as pleasant and melodic as most senior Denizens.

"And to you, Friday's Dawn," said Arthur. "I trust you heard my offer correctly? That if you will obey my orders, I shall place you in command of Binding Junction and the Top Shelf?"

"I did, Lord Arthur, and . . . reluctantly . . . I accept," said Dawn.

"Reluctantly?" Arthur asked. This Denizen was a straight talker, which made a pleasant change after Jakem.

"Yes, milord," Dawn replied stiffly. "However, I see little choice. Lady Friday has abandoned us, as have my compatriots, her Noon and Dusk. Since I am not one to partake of her . . . amusements . . . she clearly chose to leave me behind. My loyalty is thus not to Friday but to the Middle House and those in it. That is why I have resisted the invasion by Saturday's forces. The choice, as I see it, is between Saturday and yourself, Lord Arthur. I choose your service."

"I am the Rightful Heir, you know," said Arthur.

"Yes, sir, if you say so. Are you ready to accept my allegiance?"

"I am." Arthur's mind flashed back to the treacherous Pravuil, in the coal cellar, so long ago — or so it seemed. Pravuil had offered allegiance, but he'd never actually sworn it, probably because he'd been working for Saturday or someone else all along.

I'm not making that mistake again, thought Arthur. *I know better now.*

"You must swear to serve and obey me upon this, the Fourth Key," he said, holding out the rapier so the blade touched the floor in front of Friday's Dawn.

Dawn was unfazed by this. He knelt down, clanking and creaking, and took the blade in his gauntleted hands.

"I, Friday's Dawn, do swear allegiance to Lord Arthur, and shall serve and obey him until I am extinguished or until the end of all things."

Dawn looked up at Arthur expectantly, waiting for an answer.

"I accept your allegiance, Friday's Dawn, and confirm you as commander of Binding Junction and the Top Shelf and defender of the Middle House overall."

"Thank you for your trust in me, milord," said Dawn as he stood up.

"Good," said Arthur. "Now, Dawn, we need three . . ."

Arthur paused to look at Ugham.

Now is the time to leave him behind, if I'm going to, he thought. *But he has been faithful. I have the Key, and allies. . . . He will look after Fred and Suzy. . . .*

"No, four sets of wings. I have to go find Part Five of

the Architect's Will, and I think it's up in Friday's Scriptorium."

"Immediately, Lord Arthur. Do you want wings such as my Gilded Youth wear? They would size themselves better to you, I think, than the ones the High Guild use."

"Sure. Only Ugham will need bigger wings from the High Guild. Strangely, Jakem said they didn't have any."

"I meant of the sort suitable for your excellency," Jakem blurted out. "It is true we have a moldy selection of some old, ridiculously large wings —"

"Who is next in precedence to Jakem?" interrupted Dawn.

"Milka is, sir," replied Digby. "But she is away with Lady Friday. I suppose I'm next, after her."

"Then you are presently promoted above Jakem, who is now in your place," Dawn proclaimed. "I shall expect you to organize matters more efficiently than the former Pressmaster — beginning with the procurement of wings for Lord Arthur's . . . soldiers."

"I protest!" Jakem screamed to Arthur. "Surely, Lord Arthur, you cannot allow such a travesty of —"

"Dawn is in charge," said Arthur. "Go away."

Jakem went. A few minutes later, several Denizens returned carrying a set of wings for Ugham. A few seconds after them, two Gilded Youths arrived carrying three more sets of smaller, but still equally yellow, wings.

The Gilded Youths wore the same armor as Friday's Dawn, but instead of visored helmets they had golden masks, which completely covered their faces, save for thin eye, nostril, and mouth slits. They were much shorter and slighter than the Denizens, about the same size as Arthur. Seeing them, he suddenly exclaimed, "They're Piper's children, aren't they?"

"Not exactly," whispered Fred. "They started out that way, but Grim Tuesday got hold of a bunch of them and made them into . . . well, what they are . . . for Lady Friday."

"What do you mean, 'what they are'?" Arthur whispered back. The three Gilded Youths put the wings on one of the empty chairs, saluted Dawn — who was talking to Digby — and left again.

"They're mostly armor," said Fred. "I dunno how much of the original child is left inside. Least, that's what I was always told."

"It could easily be true," said Arthur. "It's just the sort of thing Grim Tuesday would have done. By the way, have you used wings before?"

"Oh, yes," said Fred. "Only it was before we got

washed between the ears. . . . Still I expect it will come back to me. . . ."

"I hope so." Arthur's own memory had completely returned, or at least he thought it had. But then he had only a fraction of experience to recall compared to Fred, who had lived for at least several hundred years by House time, maybe more. "Well, we'd better get on with it."

Suzy helped Arthur attach his wings, which grew to size. While he flapped them experimentally, she assisted Fred and Ugham. Arthur belatedly realized that Ugham might not know how to use the wings, but when he asked, the Newnith was already going through a series of exercises with his wings that displayed far greater competence than Arthur had himself. This was because Arthur had only flown once previously, in Grim Tuesday's Pit.

"Our lord the Piper was very thorough in our training," Ugham explained. "We spent many decades in practice of all kinds, before the attack on the Great Maze."

"You'll need an escort," said Friday's Dawn, who left Digby to approach Arthur. "It has been reported that the Piper and a dozen soldiers, probably Piper's children, flew to the Scriptorium peak several hours ago, followed by Saturday's Noon and a force of Internal Auditors. Now that we have Binding Junction, I can spare forty or fifty of my Gilded Youths. I would that it were more, but far too many Denizens here are experiencing."

"I don't like this experiencing business," said Arthur. "I'm not sure I really get it. Where do these experiences come from?"

"Lady Friday takes them from mortals, Lord Arthur," Friday's Dawn explained. "She partakes of most of their good memories and leaves the bad. The Denizens who are with her in her retreat fix the discarded memories on sorcerously charged paper and bring them back here to sell. Though they are usually sad and depressing memories, they are fascinating to many Denizens. You see, we do not dream, and our lives have a fixed purpose. The mortal experiences are very attractive."

"Takes them from mortals. . . ." Arthur repeated quietly. "What happens to the mortals?"

"I don't know," said Dawn. "I have never approved of the practice and Lady Friday never took me to her retreat."

"Do you know where it is?"

Friday's Dawn shook his head. "Somewhere in the Secondary Realms."

Arthur stood silently for a moment, his wings twitching. Then he took out the crystal and looked at it again.

"First we find the Will," he said. "Then we get it to help us get the Fifth Key. Come on."

He started along the corridor with everyone trailing behind, then stopped.

"Uh, I don't know the way out of here. Digby?"

"Follow me, Lord Arthur," said Digby. He led the way along the corridor and out into a pleasant, open courtyard set with strange trees that had long, curled-up yellow leaves that looked almost like scales. From there they went back into another building, into a large hall that was full of small presses, workbenches, piles of documents, and at least a hundred Denizens who were lying on their backs experiencing, with pieces of sorcerous paper stuck to their foreheads.

At the end of the hall was the main gate, which was guarded by a mixed force of mutually suspicious Gilded Youths and High Guild bookbinders, the latter armed with nasty-looking spears in the shape of seven-foot-long bookbinder's needles.

Arthur got his first proper look at the Top Shelf when he stepped outside. The mountain on which the Scriptorium sat was an imposing rocky peak some miles away. It completely dominated the northern skyline and was about four or five thousand feet high, Arthur estimated. Or at least the bit that poked up from the second sky was. He knew the actual mountain extended all the way down below the Flat, and the Top Shelf was just a small plateau of the greater whole.

Apart from the fortress behind him, most of what he could see looked like a pleasant country scene. There were meadows and occasional copses of trees. Not trees that he recognized, but still identifiable as trees, even if the color and shape of the leaves and branches were a bit strange.

There were two suns in the eastern sky, which helped explain why it was so hot. Neither was particularly large, but one was much smaller than the other. Arthur knew better than to look at them directly, but the light they cast was of a similar color to that of his own Earth sun in summer.

"I have too much to attend to here and below," said Dawn. "But your escort will be commanded by Fifteen, who is one of my most experienced Gilded Youths. Fifteen, this is Lord Arthur."

"Lord Arthur acknowledged," said the Gilded Youth. His, or perhaps her, voice was soft and crackly and sounded weirdly remote, as if it came from farther away than from inside the mask. "Flight ready to launch."

"Thank you," said Arthur. He checked the crystal again. The arrow was definitely pointing to the mountain and up. "Thank you too, Friday's Dawn. Good luck with sorting out Saturday's Dusk. If all goes well, I will be able to send help soon."

Dawn saluted as Arthur flexed his wings, kicked off,

and launched into the sky. The Gilded Youths launched at the same moment, all forty of them surrounding Arthur in a star formation, while his friends were a little slower, taking off behind to fly beneath him.

It was fun to fly. Arthur enjoyed the exhilarating rush of air past his face and the powerful feel of the wings on his back. He experimentally leaned one way and then the other, hastily correcting his balance as he almost tumbled head over heels.

"These 'ere are proper wings!" shouted Suzy. "Not like those Ascension Wings we 'ad in the Pit. Got to treat them more careful like, 'cos they go down as well as up."

Arthur had forgotten the wings he'd used before were ones that only went up.

I should have remembered that, he thought. *Those ones were stuck on with sealing wax too. These have just connected through my paper coat. I guess the washing between the ears has affected my memory. . . . I wonder what else I've forgotten. . . .*

As an experiment, Arthur tried to remember all his family's faces. He was relieved when the memories came, clear and sharp. His house was also clear, and the new school. . . .

A wind buffeted him, interrupting his thoughts. Arthur instinctively corrected and laughed aloud as he was swept up by an updraft, his wings stretching wide. The Gilded Youth called Fifteen flew near and called out in its odd, penetrating voice.

"Upwind positive. Target achievement in forty minutes."

"Thanks!" said Arthur. He looked up. The mountain peak looked as high as ever, but he could see something built on top of the bare rock. The hint of a roof.

Arthur took out the crystal again and checked it. This time, he looked at it twice and held it up even closer than before.

"Hey!" he said. "The gold arrow is pointing across now, not up to the Scriptorium. But there's nothing . . . oh . . ."

There was something. There, in the side of the mountain, about halfway up, was a small vertical crevasse, a slit in the rock that hinted at dark caverns behind.

Arthur slipped one wing down and flew around in a gentle curve to take a better look. Everyone else followed, with some of the Gilded Youths going above Arthur and some below.

"Entrance Winged Servants Night home," crackled Fifteen. "Entry forbidden day flyers."

"The arrow is definitely pointing there," said Arthur. He flew closer and hovered like a hummingbird in order to peer in the crevasse. It was only the height of a door and half as wide, and there was no ledge or step to stand on, so it would be very difficult to enter. "How do the Servants fly in?"

Suzy came to hover next to him, and Ugham and Fred hovered above.

"You'd have to fly at it and fold your wings at the last minute and kind of dive through," she said finally, and did a quick loop below. It was hard work to keep hovering.

"Forbidden day flyers," reiterated Fifteen.

"You'll never fit through there, Ugham," said Arthur. "I guess Suzy, me, and Fred will have to go alone. I hope the Servants are still feeling friendly."

"They were a bit funny about their secret eyrie," said Fred cautiously.

"I have to go in." Arthur looked at the crystal again. The tiny arrow was pointing directly at the crevasse. "Part Five of the Will is in there somewhere."

"My duty is to stay with Suzy and Fred," said Ugham. "Yet the way is too narrow for such as I am."

"I'll go in alone," said Arthur. "This is going to be tricky. Ah, Fifteen, can you and your . . . um . . . people circle here for a while, till I come back out?"

"Arthur commands is done," replied Fifteen, and turned away, the other Gilded Youths following as she flew in a wide circle out from the mountainside and back again.

"I'll be as quick as I can," said Arthur. "Keep an eye out for the Piper or Saturday's Dusk flying back down from the Scriptorium."

"We will," rumbled Ugham. He flew away from the mountain too, to join the circling of Gilded Youths. But Suzy and Fred did not.

"Quick!" said Suzy. "Let's get in before Uggie gets upset!"

Chapter Twenty

Suzy flew in a shallow dive at the narrow crack, folded her wings beautifully, and slid through, disappearing from sight, though a loud "Ouch!" announced that she had landed somewhere inside.

Arthur and Fred tried to go at the same time, Arthur only just flapping back as he saw they would collide. Fred mistimed his entry and a dozen tip-feathers of his left wing exploded into the air like blown petals as they caught on the edge of the crack.

Arthur flew in almost immediately after Fred. He managed to fold his wings properly but was going too fast. He landed at a run and then his legs buckled under him and he fell forward, striking the rocky ground on his elbows and knees, losing some skin under his paper clothes.

"Dark in here," said Suzy, somewhere in the gloom. "Do you mind if I light my wings up, Arthur?"

"Not too much. We don't want to hurt the Servants."

Suzy muttered something and her folded wings began to emanate a soft, warm glow. Fred opened his mouth to ask his wings to shed light too, but Arthur interrupted.

"Just Suzy's for now, Fred. Are your wings all right, by the way? You lost some feathers on the way in."

"Did I?" Fred twisted around, trying to look at his own back. "I think they'll still work. I suppose I won't know till I try to fly. . . ."

"At least there's plenty of people outside to catch you," said Arthur. "We'd better remember to warn them, though, when you're coming out. Suzy, can you see a way ahead?"

"Yes," said Suzy. "We're in a kind of tunnel. It's narrow and winds around a bit, but we can get through."

She took a few steps and Arthur heard a splash.

"Wet underfoot too," said Suzy. "Lots of puddles."

They followed the tunnel for at least a hundred yards, going ever deeper into the mountain. It got wetter too, water dripping from the walls and ceiling as well as pooling in puddles beneath their feet. Every twenty paces or so, Arthur checked the gold leaf crystal, and the arrow kept pointing farther in.

At last, Suzy stopped. Arthur couldn't see past her because the tunnel was so narrow.

"There's an iron gate," Suzy reported. Arthur heard her rattle it. "It's locked."

"Is there a knocker or a bell?" asked Fred.

"Don't be stupid, Fred," said Suzy. "The Servants

wouldn't put a knocker on their secret eyrie gate. . . . Hmm. . . ."

Suzy reached up and pulled something, and they heard the jangle of several bells ringing together even deeper within the mountain.

"Told you," said Fred.

"It wasn't a knocker anyway," replied Suzy. "I only said they wouldn't have a *knocker*."

"Quiet," ordered Arthur. "Someone's coming. Dim your wings a bit more, Suzy."

Suzy muttered and the light from her wings faded down to about the same luminosity as a child's night-light, hardly enough to relieve the shadows around the three of them.

"We should have gotten Fred to go first," whispered Arthur as they listened to whoever or whatever it was coming along the tunnel ahead of them. "To do the signs."

"They can hear all right," said Suzy. "And I was watching. I reckon I learned a few signs. I could try them out —"

"No!" Arthur and Fred said together. Arthur was about to add something but Suzy had started talking to a Servant the others couldn't see.

"Mornin'. Or hello again, in case we met last night. I'm Suzy Turquoise Blue and I've got Lord Arthur, the

Rightful Heir to the Architect, behind me ... and Fred, who can do your signs. Can we come through? Arthur has to find Part Five of the Will of the Architect. Thanks. By the way, have you lot ever thought about putting some drains in this tunnel? My feet are fair saturated —"

"Suzy!" whispered Arthur. "What's happening?"

"What? Oh, no problem, Arthur. Lot of nodding, a bit of hissing, and now he's going away."

"Did he open the gate?"

"Nope, but he's gone to get someone, I reckon."

"I hope you're right," grumbled Arthur. "It *is* wet in here."

No one spoke for a few minutes, then Fred suddenly said, "You know, what if this whole tunnel is a drain?"

"Fred . . ." Arthur started to say, but then they all heard the jangling of keys, and Suzy said, "Greetings."

A key turned noisily in the lock and the gate creaked open. Suzy moved forward with the others sloshing along behind. The tunnel curved to the right and began to widen. Soon all three could walk abreast, and in the light from Suzy's wings they could make out the shape of the Servant who was leading them past other tunnel openings, some of which had Servants standing in front of them, either at guard or out of curiosity to see who'd shown up.

I hope we are treated as honored visitors, thought

Arthur. *I don't know how the Key would protect me from one of their firewash projectors. I'd probably get horribly burnt but wouldn't die....*

They moved through the maze of tunnels for at least ten minutes and saw many Servants. The strange black leather-clad Denizens all had their snouted helmets on, and all of them watched silently, standing so still they might have been mistaken for statues.

At last they came to a larger space, big enough that they couldn't see the walls or the ceiling in the light from Suzy's wings. A Servant stood waiting for them. Arthur wasn't sure whether to be relieved or dismayed when he saw the moonstone claws on her gloves and recognized One Who Survived the Darkness.

The Servant who had brought them to the place bowed to One Who Survived the Darkness and edged back out. Arthur nodded, Suzy gave a salute that was actually more respectful than she usually managed, and Fred bowed.

"Greetings again," said Arthur. "I apologize for coming to your eyrie without an invitation. I have come to find Part Five of the Will of the Architect and I think it is here somewhere."

He took out the crystal and held it up. As he did so, he noticed that the arrow was now pointing down at a sharp angle.

"Oh! It was pointing here," he said. "Now it says farther down. Are there deeper levels?"

One Who Survived the Darkness made a series of signs.

Fred translated, "'You are welcome, Lord Arthur. I have long known someone would come, from my own'.... *Hmm*.... Don't know what that sign is.... My own, uh, interior?"

One Who Survived the Darkness made another sign.

"Close enough," said Fred. "Anyway, she's known you would come here."

"Oh, right," said Arthur. "Good."

"'The place you seek lies below,'" translated Fred. "'A guide will take you there to the ... Interior' ... no ... 'Inner Darkness.'"

"Thanks," said Arthur.

"'Only you, Lord Arthur, may enter the secret place of the Winged Servants of the Night, but the others may go to the entrance.'"

"Thanks," said Arthur again.

"'Your guide will take you now. May we meet again' ... uh, no ... that's actually '*maybe* we will meet again.'"

"I hope we do," said Arthur. He turned to find a Servant standing silently directly behind him, and jumped.

The Servant beckoned and turned to go. Arthur nodded to One Who Survived the Darkness and quickly followed, with Suzy and Fred at his heels.

The guide led them through yet more tunnels and tunnel junctions, and once more past many Servants. Arthur wasn't sure whether they were new ones, in which case there were an awful lot of Winged Servants of the Night inside the mountain. They all looked pretty much the same in their leather suits and snout-masked helmets.

After a while they reached a tunnel that slanted sharply down. It was barred by another iron gate, which the Servant unlocked with a key the size of Arthur's hand. After the gate there were a series of very broad steps that took them down even more swiftly, and then at the base of the steps there was an iron manhole cover that would not have looked out of place in the *Balaena*, the Raised Rats' submarine that Arthur and Suzy had traveled in under the Border Sea.

The Servant spun the locking wheel on the manhole cover and heaved it open. A wet, cold draft came billowing out, along with a curious, musty odor.

"Phew! Bit of a stink," said Suzy as she held her nose. "What's that from?"

The Servant made some signs.

"'The untrained animal,'" translated Fred.

The Servant shook his head and added some more signs and then repeated the first ones he'd used.

"Oh, right," said Fred. "The Beast. A special kind of beast . . . the Beast in the Inner Darkness, or something like that."

They all watched the Servant's hands move again, the webbing between the fingers of its black gloves stretching as its fingers flickered, signing out another message.

"'We worship it . . . we fear it. . . .'" translated Fred. "It . . . I can't quite work out this bit. . . ."

The Winged Servant of the Night repeated the signs. Fred shook his head. Then the Servant pointed at itself, put three fingers in the fixed open mouth of its sharp-snouted mask, and for the first time made a sound. A chewing sound.

"Oh," said Fred. He gulped and continued, "'Sometimes it eats one of us.' Look, I'm not sure you should go in, Arthur."

"Part Five of the Will is down there," said Arthur, checking the crystal again to make sure the arrow was pointing in the same direction. "I'm pretty . . . I'm fairly sure. I'll be perfectly safe."

"What if it's something else?"

"The Key will protect me," said Arthur. He tapped the

end of the marshal's baton. It felt comforting to know it was still there.

"It will make sure you don't get completely killed," said Suzy. "But it won't stop you from getting your leg chewed off. Slowly."

"Thanks for that reminder."

"I'd better go with you," Suzy insisted. "I'm interested in this Inner Darkness anyway. It wouldn't be a bother —"

The Servant shook his head and pointed at Arthur, then waved his open palm in a dismissive gesture in front of Suzy and Fred, before adding several other emphatic finger signs.

" 'As One Who Survived the Darkness said, only Arthur is allowed to enter the secret place of the Winged Servants of the Night,' " interpreted Fred. " 'If the Beast does not eat him, he will return safely.' "

"I'm sure it's the Will." Arthur knew that by saying it aloud he actually made himself less confident, but he couldn't help it. He only just managed not to say it several more times. "I'd better get going."

"Good luck, Arthur," said Suzy. "If the Beast does bite your leg off, or your arms, you know that I'll —"

"I know, I know," interrupted Arthur hastily, eager to forestall any more of Suzy's helpful comments.

"It'll be the Will for sure," said Fred, though his voice

cracked. He stood at attention and saluted. Arthur recognized it as the kind of ultra-snappy salute you give to someone who's going on a mission from which it is likely there will be no return.

Arthur gave a more informal wave back and turned away, mainly to hide the fear that he was sure was showing on his face. He didn't want Fred and Suzy to see that.

Under the manhole cover there was the open shaft, a vertical tunnel leading down into the heart of the mountain. The Inner Darkness of the Middle House.

"Can I illuminate my wings?" asked Arthur.

The Servant shook his head, an emphatic "no."

"Thought not," said Arthur.

The Servant paused for a moment, as if he too had to gather his courage, then he climbed into the manhole and disappeared. Arthur took a deep breath, checked the Key on his belt again, and followed the Denizen into the darkness.

Chapter Twenty-one

The ladder went a long, long way down, and after the first twenty feet there was no light at all. Even looking back up, Arthur couldn't see anything. Suzy's wings were too far from the manhole and the shaft was too narrow. He could hear the Servant below him, the metal claws on his boot tips loud on the rungs of the iron ladder.

Several hundred feet down — or so Arthur guessed — he heard the sound of those clawed boots change, and a second later his own boots found no more rungs below. There was a smooth floor for as far as he could reach while still holding on to the ladder. There was no way he was going to let go. There might be holes only feet away, or deep crevasses that ultimately might lead to Nothing.

Or the Beast itself, unseen. Waiting in the darkness.

Something touched Arthur's arm, just above the elbow. He flinched and swallowed a shriek, even as he heard the *click-clack* of claws and knew it was the Servant. The strange Denizen gripped his arm and began to lead him away, Arthur reluctantly relinquishing his hold on the ladder. The ladder that was the only hope of leaving this black hole.

Slowly, they walked deeper into the Inner Darkness. It was a cavern, Arthur presumed, but that was only because it felt and sounded like stone underfoot, and because it was inside the mountain. It might simply be a room, one cavernous enough for the echo of their footsteps to sound as if it came from far away.

Ten paces . . . twenty paces . . . thirty. . . . Arthur couldn't tell whether they were walking in a straight line or weaving a bit, the Servant gently steering him around obstacles.

Forty paces . . . fifty. . . . The Servant slowed down. Arthur heard something that wasn't just the echo of their footsteps. A soft, deep hiss like the sound of a punctured tire. A very big tire with a very slow puncture.

Breathing, thought Arthur. *Wheezy breathing from something with very, very big lungs . . .*

The Servant stopped. Arthur stopped too, swaying back from an almost-step.

"Is it here?" Arthur whispered. He couldn't help himself from gripping the Fourth Key with his left hand almost as hard as the Servant was holding his arm.

They both stood utterly still. Arthur could hear the breathing getting louder. Getting closer. He could hear his own breathing grow louder, and his heart started to beat faster, tapping out a message of fear to the rest of his body. The pulse in his neck felt as if it might break out of the skin.

Suddenly there was a mighty rush of displaced air. Arthur felt movement, close by. The Servant's grip tightened like a sudden twist of a vise, only to release an instant later as hand, arm, and indeed the whole Servant were snatched away, his still-closed fingers ripping through Arthur's paper coat, paper shirt, and skin.

Arthur cried out, but the Denizen did not. He made no sound and for a few seconds all Arthur could hear was the breathing of the Beast.

Then it began to chew. The awful sound of a particularly rude dinner-table companion, magnified many times.

It was too much for Arthur to bear in the darkness. It was too much not to know exactly what was making the awful noise.

He didn't think it through, or consider his vow not to use sorcery, didn't think he could have his wings shed light. Fear of the unknown, fear of the dark, was as deeply implanted in his psyche as in any human's, and he couldn't take any more.

He drew the Fourth Key completely from its sheath and held it high, speaking in a shrill and shaking voice that he barely recognized as his own.

"Light! Give me lots and lots of light!"

The Key began to glow with a soft, golden radiance, then before Arthur could do more than half-glance away and lid his eyes, it exploded into brilliant white light, brighter than any electric light Arthur had ever switched on, with his face effectively only inches from the source.

Something out in the former darkness shrieked so loudly the noise hurt Arthur's ears. It was a frantic *Kee-kee-kee-kee* of extreme discomfort, pitched at a tone that would have surely shattered glass if there had been any present.

Arthur tried to see what was shrieking but he was as blinded by the light as he had been by the dark a moment before.

"Less light!" he shouted urgently, focusing his thoughts on the Key. "Much less light!"

Slowly the brilliance ebbed. Arthur shielded his eyes with his right forearm and looked around. He was in a truly vast cavern of pallid green stone, and his stomach flip-flopped to see that the iron ladder came straight down the middle of it, stretching up into thin air farther than the light illuminated.

The Beast was only twenty yards away, lying on a bed of thousands of multicolored pebbles. It was shielding its head too, but with one enormous, leathery wing that stretched from the wrist of a russet-furred forearm to the ankle of blue-scaled leg. It was about forty feet long and to Arthur's eye looked to be a weird mixture of bat and dragon.

It was lizardlike from the waist down, scaled in blue iridescence, with a long, club-ended tail. From the waist up, it had red fur like a fox, and its wings were pale black and partially transparent, the bones very obvious, like struts in an old biplane's paper wing.

It had huge, pink, four-fingered taloned paws, so dextrous they could almost be hands.

In its left paw, it held the Servant, now looking like a normal Denizen, albeit one in a pale red one-piece undergarment with attached socks. He had been stripped of wings, helmet, and flying suit. All those items were in the Beast's right paw, scrunched up into a ball.

Arthur stared as the creature slowly lowered its shielding wing to reveal a fierce, foxlike head with huge, round eyes of limpid brown and a long, tapered mouth replete with rows and rows of sharp, narrow teeth.

Arthur stared even more as he saw the collar around its neck. Or, to be exact, the silver, sharp-tined crown that was welded in place, the points blunted under the Beast's chin. It made the creature look like some bizarre heraldic creature. A loose chain led from the crown-collar off into the dark.

The Beast opened its mouth wide, and Arthur forgot the crown. But before he could even think of doing anything, it suddenly threw up one hand and snapped down on what it had been holding, jaws closing with a resounding snap.

"Stop!" yelled Arthur. "Don't eat him!"

His commanding voice faltered as he saw that the Beast had in fact only swallowed the Servant's clothing, as a second course to the wings, which it had obviously eaten first.

"I wasn't going to," protested the Beast. It had a curiously high-pitched voice that made it sound a bit like a small child. "I never do. Though I must say I like the wrappers. Still, everything in moderation."

It carefully laid the Denizen down on the colored stones, which shifted under him like beans in a beanbag. As the creature moved and the light shone through its wing, Arthur saw lines and lines of type moving within the membrane between the bones.

"You are Part Five!" he exclaimed, relief making his voice squeak, so he sounded a bit like the Beast himself. "Of the Will, I mean."

"Of course I am, dear boy," said the Beast.

"I'm Arthur. That is, the Rightful Heir to —"

"I know, I know. I wondered when you would finally get here."

"Oh," said Arthur. "You knew I was here?"

"One Who Survived the Darkness talks to me a little," the Will replied. "Very tough Denizen, she is. Most of them can't go back to the Eyrie. Some deep psychological thing once the mask and leather comes off."

Arthur looked at the unconscious Denizen.

"What happens to them, then?"

"They wander down through the hidden ways and take up other employment," said the Will. "A lot of them become Paper Pushers on the canal. Now, if you wouldn't mind removing my chain? I believe there is a lot of work to be done, and while too much work is to be discouraged, I believe a fair amount should be essayed each and every day."

"Okay," said Arthur. He walked over to the Will, which was quite difficult since the pebbles kept slipping under his feet. "What's with all these little stones?"

The Will looked down at the stones.

"A hobby. I've made one for every week of my confinement here. They do add up, don't they? I suppose I should not have kept at it, but it is generally very dull down here in the Inner Darkness. Friday used to come and talk to me too, once upon a time, but I believe she has developed other interests in more recent times."

"You could say that," said Arthur. He reached up and

touched the chain to see what it was made of and whether there was any chance of breaking or releasing it without using the Fourth Key. But as his fingers touched the metal, the links simply fell apart, though the crown-collar remained around the Will's neck.

"Excellent! The touch of the Rightful Heir is true," said the Will. "I'm so glad you're not an imposter. I really didn't want to eat you."

"I appreciate that," said Arthur. He was beginning to like Part Five of the Will. It appeared to be much more relaxed than the other parts and more normal . . . considering it was a giant bat-dragon monster.

"Now tell me your doubtless fiendishly cunning plan," said the Will. It flexed its wings, nearly buffeting Arthur into the pebbles. "Pardon me. A little stretch before I resize. It has been most troublesome not being able to shrink all this time."

"My plan . . ." said Arthur. "My plan . . ."

His mouth stayed open as the Beast shrank before his eyes, going from a forty-foot-long monster to a strange-looking critter the size of a handbag poodle in a matter of seconds.

"Too small?" asked the Will. It jumped to Arthur's shoulder and let out a squawk like a parrot, which sounded very odd from a russet bat's mouth. Its draconic tail hung down Arthur's back and made him ticklish. "Mind if I ride? Flying is all very well, but not for extended periods. Now tell me the plan."

"The plan is . . ." Arthur began. "Not much of a plan. Lady Friday has supposedly abdicated —"

"She hasn't," said the Will. "Not officially. For it to be official, she'd have to tell me, and she hasn't."

"Has she left the Key in her Scriptorium for either me, the Piper, or Saturday to claim?"

"She hasn't done that either," said the Will. "The Key's not even in the House. It's out in the Secondary Realms somewhere. I can feel it."

"Um, well, the Piper and Saturday's Noon have gone up to the Scriptorium to get the Key," said Arthur. "Hopefully they've killed each other. I was planning to go up and see what was what, with a force of Gilded Youths, but . . ."

"But what?" asked the Will. "Sounds like a good plan to me. Simple. You don't want too much complexity in a plan. Nice and straightforward. Let's get going."

"If the Key's not even there, why bother?" said Arthur. But he started clambering back to the ladder.

"Might find out something useful," said the Will. "I've

got a feeling we should take a look anyway. Friday's obviously gone off the deep end. No knowing what she's done. How's the rest of me doing, by the way?"

"The rest of you?" Arthur looked around as if there might be some errant tail or other missing bit.

"Rest of the Will!"

"Oh, Dame Primus," said Arthur. "Fine, I think. Only since Part Four joined up, she's been a bit . . . vindictive."

"*Hmm*, interesting," said the Will. "Well, I'm bound to be unbalanced without me, if you know what I mean."

"No, I don't," Arthur admitted.

"Moderating influence," said the Will. "Calming temperament, that sort of thing. Known for it, you know. Got any other Keys with you, by the way? I mean left them upstairs or whatever? I can only sense the Fourth at your side."

"That's it," said Arthur. "Dame Primus wields the others as my deputy. She's got my *Compleat Atlas* too."

"*Hmm,*" said the Will. "Still, it's unlikely I would do anything really unbalanced without the rest of me . . . but perhaps we should hurry. Don't bother with the ladder. Use those wings. Mind if I hold on to your ear? Hup! Hup!"

Chapter Twenty-two

With the Will's encouragement, Arthur flew back up very swiftly. His emergence from the manhole was met by some incredulity, since he'd only been gone for twenty minutes. The small beast on his shoulder was also an object of curiosity for Fred and Suzy, who Arthur quickly introduced. The absence of the Servant guide was as quickly explained, and the Will immediately set flapping off down the corridor, urging the others to follow without delay.

Their passage out of the Eyrie was unlike their silent entry. Even more Servants thronged the passage, and as the Will flew past, they kneeled down and uttered a strange keening noise in homage, with many also flapping their wings.

One Who Survived the Darkness was waiting near the exit to the outer air. She knelt before the Will, who flew over and sat on her head. The two spoke quietly — too quietly for Arthur to hear — and then the Will flew back to the boy's shoulder.

"Thank you," said Arthur, his words soon echoed by Suzy and Fred.

The Servant made a simple sign, bowed deeply, and retreated back up the passage.

"I know that sign," said Suzy. "That was good-bye."

"It was farewell," said Fred. "Which is not quite the same."

"It was 'fly far,' actually," said the Will. "With a dash of 'fly fast' — which we had best do. Perhaps I shall grow a little and shield my eyes against the sunlight."

The Will jumped off Arthur's shoulder and before it had landed, it was about the same size as the boy. It had also grown tinted inner eyelids, which it flicked up and down in a disturbing fashion.

"I'll go first," said Arthur. "Just in case. I need to warn them too, that Fred's wing might fail."

"No it won't," said the Will. "He'd have to lose a lot more feathers for that."

"I'll still go first," said Arthur. "To . . . um . . . smooth the way."

"The Gilded Youths will recognize me for what I am," said the Will, correctly interpreting Arthur's caution.

"But Ugham might not, and he's quick with a spear," said Arthur. "Wait a moment before you come out."

Ugham and the Gilded Youths were still circling outside.

Arthur stood on the edge of the crevasse and called out to them, warning them of the Will's appearance. Then he dove out, spreading his wings as he fell, to swoop back up and join the aerial company.

Suzy came next, then the Will, then Fred, all launching safely. The Will immediately began to climb up towards the Scriptorium on the peak. Arthur followed it, with Suzy and Fred flapping strongly to catch up — and to stay away from Ugham, who swooped over to them and cast reproachful looks without openly berating them for running out on him. The Newnith had a strong practical streak, thought Arthur. He would try to fulfill his duty but didn't obsess over past infractions. Or so Arthur hoped.

A few hundred feet short of the peak, the Will slowed down and twisted around.

"Preparation is the first part of practice!" it called back.

"What?" asked Suzy.

"Ready weapons," ordered Fifteen, taking out a short, deeply curved bow from the case at her side and a stubby arrow from the sheath on her leg. "Notch arrows."

Forty Gilded Youths followed her example in smooth motion.

"Ten high, ten left, ten right, ten with," commanded Fifteen. The Gilded Youths split into groups as ordered, ten of them staying with Arthur and their leader.

The Scriptorium didn't look like much, Arthur thought as they reached the mountaintop and climbed up still higher before swooping down. There was a flat place the size of a tennis court on the very crest, and on that small area was a round, onion-domed building. The dome was gilded, which was somewhat impressive, but the foil had flaked off in many places to reveal the wooden tiles underneath. The walls were yellow plaster and they too needed repair. The building had no obvious windows.

There were a lot of bodies clustered around the single door. Arthur hovered, looking for any Piper's children that he recognized. But the bodies were all Denizens, presumably Saturday's Internal Auditors. They were dressed in black nineteenth-century-style long coats and wore long powdered wigs. Most clutched swords whose blades looked like enlarged and elongated fountain pen nibs.

"No match for the Piper," said Suzy.

"Indeed," said the Will. "The Piper is a most powerful individual. But we have me, and Lord Arthur has a Key. Onward!"

It swooped down, landing in front of the door. One of the Internal Auditors who had been lying there, apparently dead, immediately jumped up and pointed his sword, more like a gun than a medieval weapon. The Will chuckled and dived under the stream of Activated Ink that sprayed from the nib. Then he leaped up and bit the Auditor on the elbow. The Denizen sighed, dropped his weapon, and then dropped himself like a boneless fish.

"One way to do it," said Suzy, clearly impressed.

Arthur landed in a whirl of wings and Gilded Youths. Ten stayed aloft as the others came down and formed up around him, Fred, and Suzy. There were so many of them standing so close that Arthur had trouble getting to the door, which the Will was already going through.

The Piper was waiting for them inside, standing alone in a ring of dead Piper's children and the motionless body of a superior Denizen, one who had once worn the immaculate clothes of a Victorian dandy, his dark red waistcoat stained with his own blue blood. A broken ebony stick lay at his side, his smashed-in top hat next to it.

The Piper's children were the ones who had gone with Arthur on the ill-fated raid to stop the Spike in the Great Maze. Arthur recognized them immediately: Quicksilver, Gluepot, Yellowbristle, Awning, Halfcut, Sable, and Ermine.

The Piper's own yellow greatcoat was rent in several places as if torn by weapons, but there was no sign of him being actually wounded. His steel mask hid his face as always, abetted by the Napoleon hat of black oilskin. He held his wooden pipes in his gloved right hand. His left hand was also gloved, but empty.

Beyond the Piper, the room was empty, save for a slim spire of dark stone that rose up to waist-level. On it sat a shining silver mirror that Arthur knew was supposed to be the Key.

One of the Piper's children on the floor moved. Arthur took a breath, only in that second noticing that he had not been breathing.

"They're alive!" said Fred.

"Saturday's minion overrated his power to kill against my own," said the Piper easily. His voice was almost as melodious as it had been before Part Four of the Will had spat acid at him.

He inclined his head to Arthur. "I see you have once again brought the thing that calls itself the Will against me, Arthur."

"It's a different part," Arthur replied. He didn't take his eyes off the Piper, though he wasn't sure what he would, or could, do if he raised his pipes. "I didn't know what Part Four was going to do. I'd told it not to do anything poisonous."

"I suppose you expect to claim the Fifth Key too?" said the Piper.

"I will," said Arthur. "But that's not the Key. Friday's tried to trick us into fighting each other. It's kind of worked too."

"You say that is not the Key?" asked the Piper. "But you are here, with the Will and a force of lovely Gilded Youths. They are fine, are they not? They are mine too, you know, in essence."

The Piper's words were not just words. Arthur could almost see the power in them, and he saw Fifteen flinch as the Piper spoke.

"Yes, ultimate master Piper," said Fifteen. The Gilded Youths with her breathily echoed her words in a whispered chorus.

"Not to mention Banneret Ugham," continued the Piper. He made a small motion with his left hand, and Ugham strode over to the Piper's side.

Arthur kept his gaze on the Piper.

One lunge to the heart, he thought, *if he raises the pipes —*

"This is all rather tedious and besides the point," said the Will. "That isn't the Key, you know. Moreover, it is almost certainly a trap of a very nasty kind. We would all do better to leave and carry on whatever we must discuss outside."

The Piper ignored the Will.

"Ugham, fetch me the mirror from that stand of stone."

"Don't," said Arthur. "It's a trap. Besides, if it was the Key, it would kill you!"

Ugham nodded. "We know that our prince loves us not, save that we serve him. But he made us, and that is not a debt easy to repay. We serve with what honor we may retain. One slight matter remains, before I take up yonder —"

"I said to pick up that mirror, Ugham," interrupted the Piper. He had not moved, the steel mask facing Arthur, the dark holes where eyes might lie in line with Arthur's gaze.

"You do not wish to hear of a matter of import, milord?" asked Ugham.

"Get on with it!" said the Piper, his voice cracking.

Ugham nodded again, bent down, and put his spear, knuckle-duster knife, and sword on the floor. Then he reached inside his coat and put a small, folded piece of paper under the knife. Standing up, he looked Arthur in the face, and his third eye, above his forehead, winked.

"Don't do it, Uggie!" said Suzy. She started forward, but Arthur grabbed her elbow and hauled her back.

"Wisely done, Arthur," said the Piper. His voice was smooth again, but so loaded with menace that Arthur felt like he was in a room with a bomb. He had no idea of the

Piper's full powers but he wasn't confident about taking him on, even with the Fourth Key and the Will at his side. Not with the Gilded Youths arrayed against him as well.

Not to mention one sound of that pipe and Suzy and Fred will be stopped cold, Arthur thought.

Ugham saluted the Piper, but the salute also encompassed Arthur, Suzy, and Fred. Then he quickly strode over to the stone plinth, reached over, and picked up the mirror.

There was no immediate result. Ugham's shoulders relaxed a little, he took half a step back, he began to turn — and the stone floor beneath his feet groaned and shifted and then it wasn't there, an area ten feet in diameter replaced by a whirling vortex of Nothing.

In the instant the floor disappeared, Ugham was destroyed. He had no time to react or cry out; he was instantly dissolved into the pure darkness of Nothing.

Everyone else in the room only had a few seconds more. The vortex spun wider, stones falling into it as it spread.

The Piper was the first to react. With his pipes he sketched steps in the air, creating an entrance to the Improbable Stair. He jumped onto it as the floor beneath his feet ceased to exist.

Everyone else, including most of the unconscious Piper's children on the floor, was suddenly swept out of the way by an enormous scaly tail. Knocked head over heels, Arthur found himself being dragged over a knocked-down wall as the Will simultaneously grew large, smashed the wall down, and pulled the contents of the room, including Arthur, to temporary safety.

But it was only a brief respite. The vortex was still expanding. Gilded Youths sprang into the air in a panic around Arthur as he struggled to his feet. Suzy was trying to pick up Quicksilver, and Fred had his arms around Sable, his wings flapping in a frenzy.

"The Key, Arthur!" roared the Will. "Use the Key. This is a breach into the Void itself!"

Chapter Twenty-three

Arthur balanced on the very edge of the mountain, his wings extended, and raised the Fourth Key. It stayed in its baton shape, but shone with an internal light that reflected back from the crocodile ring, more gold than silver.

The vortex spread towards Arthur. Almost the entire top of the mountain was a dark absence now, and Arthur instinctively knew that as the breach into the Void spread outwards it also expanded down, eating the substance of the House.

He concentrated on the vortex and on the Key, building a picture in his mind of how it had looked when he'd flown up only minutes before.

"Be as you were," he said. "The House rebuilt, the Nothing banished."

The Key grew hot in his hand but the Nothing continued to spread, though more slowly.

I can't do it! thought Arthur, panic suddenly filling him. His concentration slipped. The Nothing began to spread more quickly, smoothly destroying everything as it lapped towards his feet. *The Fourth Key isn't strong enough in the Middle House! I need the Fifth Key and I haven't got it!*

You can do it, you know, came a thought, directly into his head. He knew it was Part Five of the Will and though it was only a mental touch, the Beast still sounded calm and relaxed. *You're Lord Arthur, you know. Wielder of Four Keys, though you might only hold one in your hand. Think of them all as being with you. Combined, they will have more than power enough.*

Arthur grimaced and imagined the clock-hand sword of the First Key, heavy at his side. The rough feel of the gauntlets of the Second Key on his hands. The trident of the Third Key at his belt, and the heavy baton of the Fourth Key in his strong right hand.

"Begone!" instructed Lord Arthur, and the Nothing was gone, and the mountaintop was all bare, polished stone, save for a rim of debris around the edge, where the Will had swept as much as it could with its tail.

Arthur blinked and looked at his hands. He *was* actually wearing the gauntlets of the Second Key. The clock-hand First Key *was* at his side. The Third Key *was* thrust through his belt.

"How . . . how did I do that?" he whispered.

"Don't ask me," said Suzy as she landed at his side. "But I reckon Dame Primus is going to be pretty miffed."

"I think I will understand the circumstance," said the Will as it landed on Arthur's shoulder, parrot-sized once more. "Once I can get together with myself. That breach could have destroyed the whole Middle House."

"Right," said Arthur dazedly. "I have to stop saying that, don't I? Particularly when I mean *wrong*. . . . Ugham's dead. . . . The Piper's children . . ."

"Quicksilver and Sable are here," said Fred somberly, who was crouched by the two children. "They seem to be just asleep. But the others . . ."

He gestured at the shallow, smooth-walled crater that had been carved by the Nothing breach.

"The Gilded Youths?" asked Arthur. He couldn't see them anywhere above.

Fred pointed down. Arthur looked. Way below there was the glint of gold and many small, distant figures.

"Flying home," said the Will. "Confused. Best place for them, really. No place like home."

"Yes," said Arthur bitterly. He looked at the crocodile ring on his finger, watching the progress of the gold with resignation. "Not that any of us will be going home."

"Where are we going?" asked Fred.

"We're going after Lady Friday," said Arthur. "To get the Fifth Key."

"We going to do like the Piper?" asked Suzy eagerly. "No elevators for us, Front Door locked, telephones off . . ."

"We will take the Improbable Stair to Monday's Dayroom," said Arthur. "Then the Seven Dials to wherever Friday is, out in the Secondary Realms. I'll use the Atlas to find her."

"But you don't want to use the Keys," said Fred.

"No," said Arthur. "I don't want to. Ugham didn't want to die for the Piper either, did he?"

Fred shook his head. "I don't understand," he said.

"I suppose you could call it honor," said Arthur. "Or responsibility, or something like that. Come on. Beast, I presume you can walk the Stair?"

"If you lead me, Lord Arthur," replied Part Five of the Will. "Or allow me to ride your shoulder."

"We'd better leave wings for Quicksilver and Sable," said Arthur. He reached back and twitched his off without thinking, handing them to Fred to lay down next to the sleeping Piper's children. Suzy shed her wings too, and picked up Ugham's weapons, though only the hilt remained of his sword and a slim splinter from the spear shaft. She also took the piece of paper, shoving it deep in an inside pocket.

Fred took his damaged wings off, but as only two needed to be left, he folded his up and put them in his pocket.

"Let's go, then," said Arthur. Using the Fourth Key, he confidently sketched steps out beyond the mountainside, and equally confidently stepped out, apparently into the empty air. Suzy followed at once, holding the back of his belt. Fred hesitated, almost lost his hold on Suzy's coat-tails, and jumped badly.

All three, with the Will on Arthur's shoulder, vanished and were gone from the Middle House.

Chapter Twenty-four

Leaf woke slowly. For several moments she thought she was in the middle of some not-very-pleasant dream, imagining she was awake. But as her senses came fully together, she knew it was no dream.

Harrison's anxious face loomed just above her own. He had the silver spoon in his hand, some noxious-looking blue liquid dripping from it.

"Wake up!" he urged. "Wake up!"

Leaf slowly edged her head up and wiped her mouth with the back of her hand. Her arm felt like it had just recovered from a bad case of pins and needles and she almost smacked herself in the lip. She was not surprised to see the smear of the blue medicine on her hand.

"What?" she said muzzily. "Who —"

"It's Harrison! Wake up! We have to go hide!"

Leaf sat up properly. Her poor, stressed brain was putting everything together.

Harrison — sleepers — Lady Friday — experiencing — Friday's Noon . . .

"What's happening?" she asked. She meant to sound incisive but her words came out slurred. Her mouth was still recovering too.

"Lady Friday's gone completely mad!" shrieked Harrison. "She's experiencing everyone! All the sleepers at once! We have to hide!"

"All the sleepers?"

"Every mortal in the place! The Denizens are putting *everyone* in the crater. They'll be here in a minute!"

Leaf looked around. She was in a room full of sleepers, much like the Yellow Preparation Room, though this room had pink walls.

"This is the last ward!" gabbled Harrison. He grabbed Leaf's arm and pulled her off the bed. "Come on!"

"Why help me?" Leaf asked groggily as she let herself be led to the door. "Why not just save yourself?"

"I said I'd help, didn't I?" Harrison said nervously. He opened the door and looked up and down the corridor. "Come on!"

Leaf followed. She was still trying to get a grip on walking as well as thinking. The two came together reasonably well after a few paces, but as her thinking improved, Leaf suddenly stopped.

"My aunt Mango!" she exclaimed. "I have to get her!"

"She's already in the crater! Everybody is," Harrison said as he ducked into a stairwell. "They'll take the sleepers in the Pink Prep Room anytime now. Hurry!"

Leaf followed Harrison down the stairs.

"We have to stop Lady Friday," she said. "She can't —"

"She *can*," said Harrison. "She *is*. Nothing we can do about it except hide and hope we survive."

"Why is she doing this?" asked Leaf. "How long have I been out?"

"Why? I don't know! It all happened suddenly. Axilrad got the order. I . . . I started to help and then I realized 'every mortal' meant me as well. Oh, you've been under for only six or seven hours. No harm done, I'm sure."

"We have to get weapons and head for the crater," said Leaf. "If we can distract Lady Friday at least —"

"We'll be killed!" said Harrison. "Use your head. We'll be lucky if we can save ourselves. Wait! Where are you going?"

"The crater," said Leaf. "There must be something I can do."

"You'll get caught up," hissed Harrison. "You'll get experienced. You're as crazy as Friday!"

"Thanks for waking me up," said Leaf. "At least you've done one good thing."

"And that's it!" Harrison turned away from Leaf and clattered down the stairs.

I need a bow or a gun or even a slingshot, thought Leaf. *Something to shoot at Friday when she hops on that rock, something to distract her long enough to run out. . . . No, that won't work. . . . I suppose Harrison is right. . . .*

Angry tears welled up at the corner of her eyes. Leaf knuckled them away as she climbed up the steps. She didn't have a clear idea of what she was going to do, but she knew she had to do something. Throw a rock from up above, perhaps, though she doubted she could throw anywhere near far enough to reach the middle of the lake.

At the next level, which she noted was circle eight, Leaf pulled out the Mariner's medallion.

"This is probably the last time I'll ask for help," she said. "If you don't come soon, it'll be too late. Lady Friday's experiencing everybody. Everything's gone wrong. I need help *now*!"

The medallion remained a lump of carved bone in her hand. Leaf tucked it in and continued to head up. A vague notion was forming in her mind. If all the Denizens were busy herding sleepers into the crater, then circle ten would be empty. There was a reasonable chance she might find something useful in Noon's office. Some kind of weapon. A replacement telephone. *Something.*

Or I might find Friday's Noon again. Leaf shivered and

forced herself to take another step, keeping close to the wall and what little shadow there was under the gaslights.

Circle Ten was as quiet as it had been before, which gave a false sense of security. There could be any number of Denizens about to pop out of their rooms. Leaf crept as quietly as she could, counting off the numbers over the doors.

She was just passing the nine o'clock mark when she saw something move right on the curve, at the eleven. If she hadn't been so nervous, she might have missed it, for it was low and small and moving slowly.

A gray-green tendril, the tip of an ambulatory seedpod. It quested about from side to side, and more of it slid into view, the thicker parts, closer to the body of the plant.

Leaf stopped and slowly began to back down the passage. She had only gone a few paces when she caught sight of another tendril, this time behind her. She was caught between two of the plants, and they were between her and the stairs.

The girl held her breath and very slowly edged over to the nine o'clock door. She gripped the handle and began to turn it, but it only moved a fraction before she met resistance. It was locked.

Leaf looked up at the gaslight above, thinking that perhaps if she could grab the pipe and point it, she could use it like a flamethrower. But there was no visible pipe, just the dragon head of the gas jet, a solid lump of bronze set into the ceiling.

The nearer tendril stopped its questing and suddenly, sickeningly advanced, rippling like a snake as it headed straight for Leaf.

Leaf shut her eyes and remembered Milka's words.

Count yourself lucky that you mortals die easily.

A terrible crackling noise filled the air and Leaf felt an excruciating pain shoot through every bone in her body, including her teeth and skull. She screamed and fell to the ground.

"Set the dials, Sneezer," said Arthur. He stood outside the circle of clocks, still clad in his paper-patchwork clothes, still bearing all Four Keys. After their arrival via the Improbable Stair — which had gone better than Arthur had expected, with only one strange stop along the way — there'd been no time to change or do anything except have a hasty conference with Dr. Scamandros, who now stood behind him, along with Part Five of the Will, Suzy, and Fred. Sneezer, the butler, stood within the circle of the seven grandfather clocks, turning the hands to the setting he and Scamandros had worked out for Lady Friday's retreat.

"You're sure Leaf didn't mention my mother?" Arthur asked again.

"Definitely not, no," replied Dr. Scamandros. "She had very little time. I fear for her."

"So do I," said Arthur. "Any luck with the telephone to Dame Primus?"

Dr. Scamandros shook his head. "Nor with telegrams. They keep coming back marked *Return to Sender*."

"The dials are set for watching, sir," said Sneezer as he retreated back out of the circle. "May I suggest you take a few minutes to look before going through?"

"Only long enough to make sure it's not opening into Nothing," said Arthur. "I don't want to waste any time. Anything could be happening to Leaf and my . . . the other mortals."

As he spoke, a trail of white fog appeared out of the floor between the clocks and began to slowly spin around, spreading quickly till there was a slowly rotating cloud. Silver luminescence rose through the white, growing brighter as it reached the edges.

Arthur blinked, and in that blink the cloud became a window to another world. Looking through it, he saw a great crowd of people — humans — standing ahead. In front of them was a lake, and in the middle of the lake there was a stone column with a silver chair set atop it. Above the chair, a winged figure was descending . . . a very tall Denizen with extra-large yellow wings, who held something impossibly bright in her right hand.

"Sneezer!" snapped Arthur. "We need to go through right now!"

The butler jumped into the circle, so quickly that his long white hair whipped around his face and the tails of his coat leaped up almost to the small of his back. He deftly adjusted the hands of several of the clocks and jumped back out.

"Go, milord!"

Arthur and his companions moved almost as swiftly as Sneezer had, entering the circle as the clocks began to chime.

Chapter Twenty-five

"**G**et up, young miss."

Leaf opened one eye. She was lying on the floor. She lifted her head slightly to see if there was a tendril poking through her chest — or some hideous botanical growth implanted in her flesh, to kill her slower than Milka had thought.

There wasn't. There was no sign of the seedpods at all. There was, instead, a very tall old man with white hair and a white three-day growth on his chin. His piercing blue eyes were fixed on Leaf. He wore a knee-length blue coat, blue breeches, and sea-boots folded over at the knee. In his hard-knuckled right hand he gripped a nine-foot-long harpoon that glittered with a light painful to Leaf's eyes.

"Captain!" sobbed Leaf. "Sir!"

The Mariner bent down and hauled her up by her elbow. "We'd best move sharp-ish," he said. "I cracked that dome when my skiff landed and all manner of gardener's horrors are climbing in. Not to mention we'd best avoid Friday. She'll not be pleased."

Leaf tried to take a breath and coughed, the cough

turning into a sob. The Mariner clapped her on the back, almost propelling her into the wall.

"That's no way for a ship's boy from the old *Mantis* to behave," he scolded. "You're safe enough now."

Leaf bit back her sobs and stood at attention.

"Begging your pardon, sir," she said, unintentionally aping her mentor, Albert. "But there are a lot of mortals who need rescuing out in the crater. Including my aunt."

"Mortals to be rescued!" exclaimed the Mariner. "I've sailed into a storm, I see. Well, let's be getting the gauge of it. Do you know of a lookout where I can espy the lay of the land?"

"There's a big window," said Leaf. "On Circle Six at about twenty past. That's down and around a bit."

"Then let's get under way," rumbled the Mariner. "And smartly."

Leaf nodded and headed for the stairs, with the Captain close behind. They did not speak for some time, but as they reached Circle Six, the Mariner laid one large hand gently on Leaf's shoulder and stopped her.

"You still have the medallion?" asked the Mariner.

"Yes, sir," said Leaf.

"You had best give it back to Arthur when you can. It was not meant to be passed into other hands."

"I'm sorry," said Leaf. "I didn't know who —"

"No harm done," said the Mariner. "But I am not without business of my own. Three times I will answer to the call. I owe young Arthur that. This is the second, and for the third and final time, the call must come from Arthur himself."

"Yes, sir," said Leaf again. The Mariner raised his hand and indicated for her to go on.

The window was where she remembered. It was clear glass or something like glass, about seven feet long and three feet high. It looked directly out on to the lake and the crater floor, a few hundred feet below.

"There," said Leaf. "All those people, the sleepers lined up on the shore. Oh! Friday's already landing on the rock. She'll use the Fifth Key to suck all the people's memories out of them. Their experiences!"

The Captain looked out — at Lady Friday alighting on the silver chair upon the rock; at the thousands of sleepers who were lined up all around the crater; at the dozen or more Denizens who circled above Friday.

"The odds are poor," he said. "But the position is good."

With that, he tapped the glass with the point of his harpoon and it flew out in a single piece, shattering on the rock far below. Leaf shuddered as a wave of pain and nausea went through her, but it was soon past. The feeling came from the harpoon, she realized, and she sidled away from the Mariner.

"Now," mused the Mariner. "I shall get perhaps two good casts before they are upon us. What, then, shall be my targets?"

Down below, Lady Friday raised her hand and the mirror that was the Fifth Key shone even brighter.

"Quick!" shouted Leaf. "She's going to —"

The Key flashed, its stark light banishing darkness from every corner and crevice within the crater. The lake and dome flicked to silver, and from the eyes and mouths of the thousands of sleepers, a mad spaghetti of colored streamers sprang out towards Lady Friday's hand. Once again she gathered them up, the mirror in her hand transforming from something of pure white brilliance to a bright rainbow that overflowed down her arm.

Lady Friday raised the mirror and tipped her head back, opening her mouth with its perfect white teeth.

"Stop her!" yelled Leaf. "Don't let her drink them all up!"

"That's Leaf's voice," said Arthur as he stumbled out onto the rocky surface of the crater, accidentally pushing over several sleepers. For some reason his balance was way off and he stumbled again before he righted himself. He could hear his friend but he couldn't see her anywhere or make out what she was shouting. All he could see was a sea of sleepers, Friday perched on her rock, and the Denizens who flew above her.

"Friday is using the Key," warned the Will, who came right after him. It shrank itself down some more and scuttled between two swaying sleepers. "In a most peculiar fashion."

"This is unusual," said Scamandros, who was next to emerge from the white-lit transition from the Seven Dials. He raised his glasses to his forehead and peered at the nearest sleeper. "These mortals are being drained of . . . well, not *life*, exactly, but close to it."

Leaf had stopped shouting. Arthur was about to push forward when he heard a distant crackling sound and a pain he knew danced across his teeth. An instant later, the Mariner's harpoon flew down from the crater wall. It looked as if it would strike Friday but she leaped up the merest fraction of a second ahead of its impact, yellow wings bursting to turn her jump into flight. The Key stayed in her hand, rainbow-bright and full of experience.

"The Mariner!" shouted Friday, pointing up at the crater wall. "Attack him!"

A dozen Denizens, including the monocled Noon,

wheeled in the air and flew towards the window where the Mariner held out a hand for his returning harpoon.

"Stop!" roared Arthur. He raised the baton of the Fourth Key high, hands steady in the gauntlets of the Second Key. "Keys, bring Friday to me! And you Denizens, leave the Mariner alone!"

Arthur's voice echoed throughout the crater. It did not sound like a boy shouting, but a great lord calling for his servants to do his bidding.

Lady Friday jackknifed in the air as she tried to fly back to her balcony. Still holding the mirror with its cargo of experience, she was carried backwards as if blown by a wind, landing in an unladylike sprawl in front of Arthur. More sleepers tumbled out of her way, but she paid them no heed.

"So, you got out," she said to the Will conversationally. "This boy managed what you could not yourself."

"That is so, madam," said the Will. "And now it is time for you to relinquish your charge to this same boy, who is not a boy at all, but Lord Arthur, the Rightful Heir."

"I am ready to do so," said Friday. "But may I just taste a little more? I am defeated, I know, but only as a mortal can I truly know the feeling of defeat. Give me just a few minutes more, let me enjoy the rich textures of mortal life once more —"

"No," said Arthur. He sheathed the baton and held out his hand. "I, Arthur, anointed Heir to the Kingdom, claim the Fifth Key —"

Friday screamed and tried to tip the mirror to her mouth, rainbow threads falling everywhere around her face. Arthur spoke more quickly, gabbling out the words.

"— and with it the demesne of the Middle House. I claim it by blood and bone and contest out of truth in testament and against all trouble!"

The mirror flew from Friday's hand into Arthur's. She shrieked again and hurled herself after it. Arthur dodged aside, hurtling farther than he intended due to the lesser gravity. Friday whirled to try again, but the Will, grown larger again, gripped the back of her neck with its sharp bat teeth and shook her till thin rivulets of blue blood ran down her shapely neck.

Arthur looked for a moment at the rainbow-hued mirror in his hand and then at all the sleepers. He felt no sense of triumph. He felt sick in his heart, hollow and defeated.

"I suppose my mom's here somewhere," he said. "We were just that little bit too late."

Dr. Scamandros coughed and raised his hand. "Ahem, Lord Arthur, I believe it may not be entirely too late. The great majority of the extracted experiences must still lie within the Key. It is possible they can be returned. Friday would know best."

Arthur turned to Friday, who hung limp and silent in the Will's jaws. "Is it possible to return the experiences?" he asked.

"Perhaps," said Friday dully. "I do not know. If it lies within the power of the Key, it can be done. I am no sorcerer."

"Arthur, the Mariner is signaling," said Fred.

Arthur looked up at the crater. He could make out the Mariner clearly now, and he felt a small surge of happiness when he saw that the small figure by his side was Leaf.

"Arthur!" roared the Mariner, his seagoing voice of command almost as loud as Arthur's sorcerously magnified shout had been. "There are dangerous plants getting in! Order Friday's Denizens to repel boarders!"

"What?" Arthur shouted back. "Dangerous what?"

"Plants!" shouted the Mariner, and Leaf too, from the look of it, though her voice was totally drowned out.

The Denizens who were circling above heard it clearly. All but one swooped down towards Arthur and for a second he thought they were going to attack. But they halted to hover a good distance away, and one of them spoke.

"Lord Arthur, may we go to fight the plants at once? If

their way in is not stopped promptly, we will be swamped."

"Go and fight the plants," ordered Arthur. Then he looked up and said, "Hey, where have Friday's Noon and Dusk gone?"

"Lord Arthur, if I may interrupt," said Scamandros. "There may be a time factor in returning the experiences. A degradation may occur if it is not done quickly —"

"Right!" said Arthur. "How do I put the experiences back?"

Scamandros looked doubtful and the tattoos on his cheeks changed from books with turning pages to a wild tangle of question marks that began to fight one another.

"The Keys shortcut much sorcery," he said. "If you assume the position Lady Friday took when taking the experiences, and simply ask the Fifth Key to replace the stolen experiences, it may work. Unfortunately, to discern a more rigorous technique would take me days or weeks."

"Give me your wings, Fred," Arthur said quickly. "Stick them on. Thanks. Don't let Friday go, Will. Suzy, keep an eye out for Friday's Noon and Dusk. They should know they're beaten, but . . ."

He flexed the wings and leaped into the air, careful to hold the Fifth Key level. He knew that it wasn't like a cup and he probably couldn't spill the contents, but it didn't hurt to be careful.

The silver chair was sunk, though Arthur could see it through the clear blue water. So he stood on the stone pillar and faced the direction Friday had. Seeing all the sleepers standing and swaying all around him, he couldn't help but search for his mother's face. Was she here? Were there other people he knew?

"Hurry!" called out Scamandros, who was looking closely at the back of one of the sleeper's heads.

Arthur took a deep breath, raised his arms as he had seen Friday do, and concentrated his thoughts on the Fifth Key. Just to be sure, he also spoke aloud, though quietly, so only he could hear.

"Fifth Key, return the experiences you hold to these poor people, so that they are just as they were before Friday stole their precious lives. Repair their memories and give back all their happinesses —"

He paused for the briefest instant, wondering whether that was all they needed, but in that same moment knew that it was not. He would not himself be content to have only his happy memories.

"— and all their sorrows. Thank you."

The Key flashed with multicolored light, and streamers

exploded out from Arthur's hand, snaking back across the silver-mirrored lake to connect with all the sleepers, making for just a few seconds a brilliant shining lattice of every color of the rainbow.

Then the streamers were gone and the mirror in Arthur's hand grew dull. As the sleepers still swayed and shuffled in their places, Arthur spread his wings and flew back to the others.

"Did it work?" Arthur shouted in dismay as he landed. "They don't look any better!"

Scamandros leaned back from the head he was inspecting, pushed his glasses farther up his forehead, and shouted back, "Yes! Most, if not all, of the stolen experience has been returned. The sleep is a different matter, merely an instruction from Friday, easily broken. But I suggest we leave them asleep until they can be returned."

"You have done well, Arthur," said the Will, who had spat out Friday and was now content to keep her wrapped under one wing. The former Trustee did not complain or struggle. She sat there, staring into space, her eyes unfocused. "Very well indeed."

Arthur was not listening. He was already aloft again, flying over the crowd, searching for his mother.

"That's a dozen gold roundels you owe me, Fred," said

Suzy. "Told you we'd get back to Arthur and get the Fifth Key before we got a decent cup of tea."

"We got a cup of tea at Binding Junction," protested Fred.

"Not a decent cup," said Suzy. "That was poison."

"I wonder how we are going to get all these people back to where they belong," said Scamandros. "And now that I think of it, I wonder how *we* are going to get back. I forgot to pack a Transfer Plate!"

Chapter Twenty-six

"**S**he's not among the sleepers in the crater," Arthur said an hour later. The silver chair had been fished out of the lake and set up on the shore, and he was sitting on it, as the centerpiece of an impromptu court or council of war. "Leaf, are you sure this Harrison fellow would know if she was here?"

Harrison, who had been found hiding in the linen store, nodded from where he was kneeling in front of Arthur. Leaf, who was sitting at Arthur's side on a wooden chair from one of the closer rooms, also nodded. Her aunt Mango stood next to her, swaying from side to side and occasionally snoring.

"Harrison had the records from Friday's hospital back home of everyone sent through. I'm on the list, but there's no mention of your mom."

"Someone else has taken her, then," said Arthur. "Scamandros, there can be no doubt she is not on Earth?"

"If we could not find her through the Seven Dials, she is either shrouded by sorcery or somewhere else," Scamandros replied.

Arthur bit his lip, then asked the question that had been worrying him for a long time.

"Could she be dead?"

"Only if no one knows she is dead. Which is very unlikely."

"I have to find out," said Arthur. "I don't suppose it's any use now, but Scamandros, if I use the First Key instead of the Fifth, will it contaminate me less?"

"No, Arthur," Scamandros said sadly.

"Thought not," Arthur muttered. He raised the mirror, glad that he couldn't see the crocodile ring and its measure of his sorcerous contamination under the gauntlet of the Second Key. "Friday, I charge you by the power of the Fifth Key to tell me truly if you know anything of what has happened to my mother since last Thursday, in the time of Earth, my home."

"I know nothing," whispered Lady Friday. "I would have taken your mother, if she had been there for the taking. But she was not among the patients of the temporary hospital from which I took my final selection. I would have so enjoyed her experiences, I'm sure —"

"Enough!" ordered Arthur.

He bent his head and kneaded his forehead with his gauntleted fingers until a sudden fear that this could somehow contaminate him even more made him sit back straight, just in time to see the Mariner approaching. He was leading two bedraggled Denizens, who were in turn carrying across their shoulders Friday's Noon and Dusk. The two superior Denizens were silent and still, their eyes closed, but they were not dead. There were papers stuck on their foreheads, hanging down over their elegant noses. Friday's Noon had lost his monocle.

"Milka and Feorin!" said Leaf. "These were the two who helped me. Not that they really meant to."

"I found them trying to sneak out and board my ship!" The Mariner laughed. "Doubtless they did not know what I do with stowaways!"

Arthur looked at the bedraggled would-be star sailors, and then at Friday's Noon and Dusk. He was annoyed that they had escaped punishment, the more so that they were doing it by partaking of some poor long-lost mortals' lives.

"Can they be brought out of their experiencing?" he asked.

"Not without breaking their minds," said Scamandros. "It is not an area which I have studied. I don't know who has. Now, Arthur, we must get these sleepers back to their Secondary Realm, to your Earth. They will wake up before too long and I doubt that waking here would serve them well."

"I need to get Aunt Mango back," confirmed Leaf.

"Easier said than done." Arthur felt the pocket at his side where the Fifth Key rested. They had already established that there were two ways out of Friday's retreat, mirror-paths set up that could be activated by the Key. One went back to the private hospital on Earth and the other to the Middle of the Middle House.

"Martine can lead us back if you can open the way with the Key," said Leaf. She had spoken to the craggy-faced, gray-haired woman, who was not anywhere near as mad as Harrison had made out. She was just shy and deathly afraid of Lady Friday and the Denizens, though she'd served the former Trustee for at least thirty years.

"I've got a Transfer Plate too," said Suzy, pulling out a disc of burnished electrum. "The doc can retune it for the Citadel or wherever you want to go, Arthur."

"I want to go back to Earth!" said Arthur. "I'm just not sure if that's the right thing to do. The Piper may already be attacking the Citadel again, and without the Keys, Dame Primus will be hard-pressed. So perhaps I should go there. Or I should move directly against Saturday . . . if I can figure out some way of getting into the Upper House. There's just so much I don't know!"

"Knowledge, like all things, is best in moderation," intoned the Will. "Knowing everything means you don't need to think, and that is very dangerous."

"Whatever you decide, Arthur, I must be away," said the Mariner. "The solar tide of this purple star flows strongly, and I would catch it. If you do not require them, I might also take these Denizens. My current ship requires no crew, but I have my eye on a larger vessel."

"They may go, if they wish," said Arthur. "Though if you could stay, Captain, I'd really appreciate it."

"Do we wish?" Feorin asked Milka.

"Definitely," said Milka. She bowed low to Arthur, and then almost as low to Leaf.

"I must catch the tide," said the Mariner. "I am a sea-farer, Arthur. Long ago I decided I did not want to be immured in all the politicking and bickering within the House. When my debt to you is fully paid, I shall not come again, save that it be at my own whim."

The Mariner saluted Arthur. Then he took his crew and left, striding back inside to begin the long climb up to the crater rim where his small starship nestled against a crack in the dome. As they disappeared, Leaf heard Feorin asking the Mariner whether he had his ship's log bound in leather or calfskin.

"I have decided," said Arthur. "I will go back to Earth with you, Leaf, and the sleepers. Suzy — you, Fred, and the Will had better use the Transfer Plate to go to the Great

Maze and take Friday with you to be locked up, with her Noon and Dusk. Dr. Scamandros, I have the plate here that took me to the Middle House. You can reset it for Monday's Dayroom — I know Dame Primus wants you to keep an eye on the Old One."

"It is not the Old One that is troubling," said Dr. Scamandros. "He is chained as always. But there has been a curious winnowing of Coal-Collaters and other strangeness in the cellars. I am investigating that."

"I am going to give you the first four Keys to take to Dame Primus," continued Arthur, directing his attention to the Beast. "I'll need the Fifth Key to get back to the House. Which I will do as soon as possible."

"I'd keep them all if I was you," said Suzy.

"No," said Arthur. "Everything of power from the House, Denizen or Key, has a bad effect on the Secondary Realms. I have brought enough plagues and troubles to my world. Besides, Dame Primus will need them to fight off the Piper. And Saturday."

"Saturday!" exclaimed Suzy. "That reminds me. Where did I put it?"

She rummaged in the pockets of her paper coat, pulled out a small square of paper, and handed it to Arthur.

"It's the paper poor old Uggie had. I reckon he got it

from the Raised Rat who used the Transfer Plate Friday sent to Saturday, the one whose tracks we saw in the snow. There's a bloody paw print on the outside, see?"

"What is it?" asked Arthur. He unfolded it as Suzy answered.

"Something worth a Raised Rat dying for, I'd say."

Arthur read what was written on the scrap of paper aloud. It had been torn from a larger paper, and there was an edge that he thought had probably once held a seal, for there was a trace of the rainbow wax used by all the Trustees.

For the last time, I do not wish to intervene. Manage affairs in the House as you wish. It will make little difference in the end.

S.

Lady Friday

Y Ni 13109

Nix, Garth.
D. A. Hurd Library March 2010

DATE DUE

JUN 1 7 2010	FEB 1 5 2012	
JUN 1 7 2010		
JUL 0 2 2010		
AUG 0 5 2010		
FEB 1 9 2011		
APR 2011		

DEMCO 128-5046